P●INT

THE BEAT

Losers

David Belbin

■SCHOLASTIC

The city in these pages is real. The events described in them are not. All of the characters, together with the police station where some of them work, are imaginary. The author wishes to thank the many people, including serving police officers, who helped him with this series. He alone is responsible for any mistakes.

Scholastic Children's Books
Commonwealth House, 1–19 New Oxford Street,
London WC1A 1NU, UK
a division of Scholastic Ltd
London ~New York ~ Toronto ~ Sydney ~ Auckland

First published in the UK by Scholastic Ltd, 1997

Copyright © David Belbin, 1997

ISBN 0 590 19010 5

All rights reserved

Typeset by TW Typesetting, Midsomer Norton, Somerset

Printed by Cox & Wyman Ltd, Reading, Berkshire

3 5 7 9 10 8 6 4 2

PROLOGUE

It was a slow night. Gary and Clare had only been on patrol for three hours, but it felt more like eight.

"So who's coming to the party next weekend?" Gary asked. "And what do you reckon people will say when they find out—"

Clare shushed him.

"Hear that?"

She wound down the window and let in the warm night air.

"I hear it," Gary said. "Shall I turn on the siren?"

"No. The burglars might still be inside."

"More likely that a spider set off the alarm."

They turned up the hill, then into a wide drive-way with wrought-iron, electrically operated gates.

"They're not usually open," Clare commented.

"You've been here before?" Gary asked.

"Only driven past it."

The house at the end of the driveway was a huge red and white monstrosity, with a swimming pool to one side and a quadruple garage to the other. The place was less than two years old and had been built on a piece of prime land that used to be a school's sports field. It was very private. It fact, it was too private. You couldn't see the house from the street and, with all the traffic noise from the ring road, it was hard for anyone to hear the burglar alarm going off.

Clare and Gary drew up in the wide driveway at the front of the house. A man stood in the doorway. He was thirtysomething, with a florid face, thinning hair and a garish summer shirt which, it became clear as they got closer, was drenched in sweat.

"What took you so long?" he said. "I set the alarm off fifteen minutes ago, two minutes after I got in."

"I'm sorry, sir," Clare said. "Is this some kind of test?"

"No test. There's been a serious crime here."

"In that case," Clare suggested, in a civil tone, "you should have telephoned."

"I couldn't," the homeowner told her, pointing at the wall. "They cut the line."

"You've been burgled?"

"Yes."

2

"They take much?" Gary asked.

"Cleaned out the place. But I don't care about that. They've got my wife."

The man identified himself as Gordon Loscoe. His wife, Gordon told them, was called Maxine. In the hallway was a frightened-looking fourteen-year-old girl, wearing pyjamas.

"This is our Natalie. I found her tied up."

"How long ago did they leave, Natalie?"

"I don't know," the girl said. "At least an hour."

Gary asked the girl a few questions, but she'd seen nothing helpful. A masked man had dragged her from her bed and tied her up. There had been at least one other.

Clare used her radio to get a message to the CID on-call officer, then spoke to Inspector Grace at the station.

"It looks like the motorway team, sir."

"I'm on my way."

A description of Maxine Loscoe went out over the radio.

"I'm sure we'll find her soon, sir," she told the homeowner.

Gordon Loscoe sat down. He was, Clare realized, rather drunk.

"Maxine. My Maxine. They've kidnapped her. I'll pay anything, all right? I won't hear any argument. I've got money for the ransom."

"We'll take it one step at a time," Clare told him, glancing around her. The house was probably the ugliest she'd ever been in. The hi-tech furniture, the embossed striped wallpaper and the deep crimson carpet must have cost a fortune, but only managed to look garish and mismatched.

"The likelihood is," Clare reassured Mr Loscoe, "that they haven't kidnapped your wife for ransom."

"How can you tell?"

"Burgling and kidnapping are different kinds of crime. You rarely get the two of them together. Tell me, do you have any accounts with cash cards for hole-in-the-wall machines?"

"A few."

"Does your wife have cards for all these accounts?"

"Of course."

"Know where she keeps them?"

Loscoe scurried upstairs. A minute later he was back.

"All gone."

Clare turned to Natalie.

"You're sure they left the house at least an hour ago?"

"Yes."

"A little before midnight, probably?"

"Yes."

"That makes sense. They can do the double."

"Pardon?" Loscoe said.

"Most cash cards have a limit on how much you can withdraw in a day. But the day changes at midnight. So, if they use each card once just before midnight and once just after, they double their take."

Loscoe swore.

"Do you mind if I ask where you were, sir? Why did you get home so late?"

"I was at the casino in Hockley. Having a bad night. Decided to cut my losses and come home. Didn't even notice anything wrong until the taxi had dropped me off."

Clare got the taxi firm's name, in case the driver might have noticed something. Then she went to see what Gary had found out. He was standing in front of a round, wooden conservatory that had been painted bright pink.

"This place is a monument to bad taste," Gary said. "You know who he is, don't you?"

"Gordon Loscoe? No. Some kind of celebrity?"

"You could say that," Gary told her. "I remember seeing him on the TV news. He used to live on the Maynard Estate. Did up old cars for a living. That was before he won three million quid on the National Lottery."

1

"Look out for missing female, IC one, age thirty, height five feet four, medium build with red hair cut in a bob. Probably wearing a green raincoat over a nightdress. Her name is Maxine Loscoe. She may be in a distressed state. Maxine is thought to have been forcibly taken to cash machines and threatened into making withdrawals."

Ben took a detour into the old Market Square. It wasn't on his beat, but it had more cash machines than anywhere else in the city. He glanced at his watch. Nearly half-past one in the morning. The taxi queue was short and the streets weren't lively. The next burst of life would come at two, when the clubs threw out. Ben saw no sign of anyone answering Maxine Loscoe's description so continued on up Friar Lane and on to Maid Marion Way.

Ben was driving solo. He was meant to be partnering Tim Cooper at the moment, but Cooper was off with back trouble, which suited Ben fine. Ben preferred working alone to having the best of partners, which Tim Cooper wasn't. Tim was cynical and full of prejudices, though if he had it in for blacks, he was careful not to let Ben know. Another call came through on the radio.

"Reports of a violent domestic on the Maynard Estate. There were complaints earlier about noise. Now a neighbour's called to say it sounds like someone's been hurt."

Ben responded.

"Have any officers already been round?"

"No. It's the Wilder house."

Ben swore. The Wilder family was trouble. Three generations lived in one tiny house. The grandmother, Shirley, had only just turned thirty. Her eldest, Julie, was sixteen or seventeen and had a young baby daughter. Both women were unmarried. Shirley had a history of violent boyfriends with criminal tendencies. Julie, Ben knew less about. She kept herself to herself, so he wouldn't know her if he saw her. The real villain was Shirley's son, Curt. Curt was fourteen or fifteen now. By the time he was thirteen, Curt had been through every secondary school in the city of Nottingham that was willing to take him. He'd tried his hand at arson, shoplifting, joyriding, vandalism and housebreaking. His school, on the rare occasions when he felt like going or had been forced to attend, was a special unit in the Meadows.

The Maynard Estate was a maze of houses with limited vehicle access. The central areas were pedestrian only, apart from a cycle path. You could just about drive a car along that – at least, you could until you hit the bollard by the shops. Curt Wilder had wrapped a Renault 5 around that bollard three months ago, after nicking the car to get home from the last Forest away game of the season.

Ben parked anxiously. He wouldn't be able to see the car from the Wilder house. He could well return to find the wheels missing, windows smashed and radio torn out. Before going in, he called to see if more officers were on their way. Jan Hunt, his sergeant, responded, but without enthusiasm. No one liked having to deal with the Wilder family.

There was music coming from the house, loud enough to keep most people awake. Maybe that was all this was. With complaints about the noise not having got a police response, the caller, who was across the road a couple of doors along, had made up some story about a violent fight. Ben knocked on the neighbour's door first, expecting some old biddy. Instead, it was answered by a man of about his own age, which was twenty-three.

"Noise been like this long?" Ben asked.

"Since about four this afternoon. They been having some kind of a party. Doesn't bother me – I stay up late myself. But twenty minutes ago, when there was a gap in the music, I heard what sounded like a fight – a woman's voice, shouting. I couldn't make out the words. The music was too loud. Then there was a crash, followed by a kind of scream."

"Could you describe the scream more precisely?"

"It was a cry of pain."

"Man or woman?"

"Can't be sure."

Ben was relieved to see Jan Hunt walking towards him, accompanied by John Farraday. As the officers approached, doors and windows along the rest of the road began to open. People came out, waiting to see the free show. Ben banged on the door.

"Police!"

Shirley Wilder opened the door with the chain on. She was a wan-faced but not unattractive woman, wearing a long T-shirt and not much else.

"All right," she said. "We'll turn it down."

"It's not about the noise," Ben said. "Can we come in, please?"

"I suppose so."

"Could you turn the music down anyway?" Jan Hunt asked politely, once they were inside.

"Curt!" Shirley yelled. "Turn that frigging noise

off!" The music stopped. A baby began crying. Or maybe it had been crying before, but they just couldn't hear it.

"May we see the other people in the house?" Jan asked Shirley.

"Why would you want to do that?"

"There've been reports of someone being assaulted."

Shirley sneered. "There are some nosy beggars around."

They followed her into the kitchen-and-dining area. The kitchen surfaces were mainly taken up by a sound system. The room reeked of booze, tobacco and dope. Curt Wilder sat at the small table, hunched over his can of lager like an ageing vagrant.

"What's been happening?" Ben asked.

Curt looked up to reveal a bruised neck and a cut arm. There was blood all over his T-shirt. He said nothing.

"Curt had an accident," Shirley told them. "He fell over."

"That's right," Curt said.

"Fell over someone's fist, did he?" John Farraday suggested, in a matey, local tone that Ben could never achieve, and envied.

"Caught his head on the door handle," Shirley replied. "Didn't you, Curt?"

"Don't remember," Curt mumbled.

"Where's your daughter?" Jan asked.

"In bed."

"We'd like to see her."

"Julie!" Shirley yelled up the stairs.

"What is it?" a male voice answered.

A youth in boxer shorts came out of the bedroom and saw Ben climbing the stairs. "Yeah?"

"We're checking everyone's all right."

"Oh, yeah?"

Ben clocked the guy's tattoos and the way his muscles made them throb. He looked like he was waiting for a chance to hit someone. Maybe he'd already hit Curt.

"You are?"

"None of your business."

"I'd like to see Julie."

"You can't go in there. She's not decent."

"I'm sure you won't mind if I go in," Jan said, pushing past both men into the bedroom, where the baby had stopped crying.

"What would you do if you won the Lottery?" Gary asked Clare.

They had been relieved by Scenes of Crime and CID, so were back on patrol, cruising the streets in the hope of finding Maxine Loscoe.

"I've never thought about it," Clare said.

"Pull the other one!"

"Honest, I've never done the Lottery, not even a scratch card. I was brought up to believe that

11

gambling corrupts the soul."

"Come on, Clare. The Lottery's a laugh. No one expects to win, but it's fun to daydream about what would happen if you did."

"And what would you do?" Clare said, playing the game to humour him.

"With three million? I'd keep working, of course. This is what I've always wanted to do with my life. But I'd buy a big house, and a Ferrari, and a new house for my mum and dad. I'd join that expensive gym in town. And I'd give half a million to Aids research. No, make that a million. And five thousand each to all my friends. I'm including you there, by the way."

"I'll hold you to that, should your fourteen-million-to-one bet pay off."

"Fourteen million to three. I buy three tickets each week: one set of numbers that I choose, one set that's always the same, and a lucky dip."

Clare smiled, enjoying Gary's optimism, and wondered why she didn't indulge herself. After all, some of the money went to good causes. And what else would two or three pounds a week buy? It wasn't even enough for a fish-and-chip supper. Maybe Clare's dislike of the Lottery had something to do with morality. But the only place she heard the word "morality" these days was in church. And she had already missed three Sundays this year.

"Do you see what I see?"

They were driving through Hyson Green, past Asda. A red-headed woman in a filthy raincoat was standing in the supermarket's petrol station, trying to hold herself up by one of the pumps.

"There are a couple of cashpoint machines by the supermarket entrance," Clare pointed out, as she drove onto the forecourt.

"Nice secluded ones," Gary commented.

The cut on Maxine Loscoe's temple was an even darker red than her hair.

"Shall we call an ambulance or take her to Casualty ourselves?" Gary asked.

"Let's get her there."

Gary helped Maxine into the back of the car as Clare radioed ahead to the hospital. Then she set off at speed, siren blaring. In the back seat, Gary tried to get some sense from the victim.

"Hit me on the head and threw me out of the car. I had to c–c–c–"

"Crawl?" Gary filled in for her.

"They made me crawl," Maxine agreed, before being sick all over Gary and the back seat.

Julie Wilder sat on the bed, breastfeeding. Her face glowed. Jan felt a tinge of envy. She had never looked so healthy when nursing Henry, her baby. Julie could be posing for a portrait of the Madonna and child.

"Is something wrong?" she asked.

"Your brother's been hurt."

"He's always getting hurt."

"How did it happen this time?"

"How should she know?" her nameless boyfriend asked.

"I'll ask the questions, if you don't mind," Jan said. "Did you see what happened?"

The question could have been addressed to either of them, but neither answered.

"What does Curt say happened?" Julie asked.

"Curt's not doing a lot of talking," Jan said.

"Well, then."

"Someone's got to give us a story better than, 'he fell and banged his eye against a door handle'."

"All right," Julie said to Jan. "We were celebrating and things got out of hand. It's over now. How's that?"

"I guess that's all there is to it," Jan told her, going to the door, glad to be getting out of the place. Then she thought about what the girl had just said.

"Celebrating what, by the way?"

"This!"

Julie reached into her purse and pulled out a scratch card, one of those where you had to match the same figure three times to win a prize. Jan looked at it. The sum of £1 appeared once; £20 appeared twice. The figure of £50,000 showed three times.

"That's right," Julie said. "I've won the Lottery."

2

"Happy birthday," Ben said to Ruth, as she climbed into his bed on Saturday afternoon, waking him up. "What time is it?"

"Two–fifteen."

He'd come off shift at six. It had taken him a couple of hours to get to sleep, so he'd had just enough rest. Ruth was on mornings this week. Now they were both off for the weekend. After taking a shower, they ate what was breakfast for Ben and a late lunch for Ruth.

"Do you want your present?" he asked her.

"I thought you'd never get round to it."

He produced two envelopes. The first contained a card, signed "With all my love". The second was equally thin.

"What is it?" Ruth asked. "A book token?"

Ben smiled. Ruth opened the envelope, took out the slip of paper, and hugged him.

"Ibiza! That's brilliant. But you can't afford it."

She was right. He couldn't. But that was what credit cards were for.

"I got your sergeant to check the holiday rota and you can have the ten days off, no problem."

Ruth looked at the travel agents' letter of confirmation again.

"When do we go? The day after the party. That's great."

"Not till the afternoon, though, so we can sleep off the party first."

"Great."

"It's only a self-catering apartment—" Ben began to say.

Ruth hugged him again.

"Don't be daft. This is the best birthday present I've ever had. I love you."

"I love you too," he said.

They kissed, then went back to bed.

"What happened after I'd left last night?" Clare asked, as she and Paul Grace finished their dinner at Sonny's, a fancy restaurant on the edge of the Lace Market. They'd avoided discussing police work all evening, swapping life histories instead. But now they were up to date, so Clare was indulging her curiosity.

"Not a lot," Paul told her. "Scenes of Crime didn't turn up anything to speak of. The wife's story was on the incoherent side. From the sound of it, she was about to head for bed when the burglars arrived. They followed their usual MO, except for the whack on the head Maxine Loscoe got being a little on the strong side."

"She'll be OK?" Clare asked.

"Hospital should be releasing her this afternoon. CID will interview her again then."

"You don't sound very hopeful."

Paul shook his head.

"A team like this, they're professionals. Local CID's only chance is a lucky break. But the burglars had been gone an hour when you and Gary showed up. They could be in Birmingham by that time, or Sheffield, or halfway to London."

"How many is it that they've done now?" Clare asked.

"I think this one takes them into double figures."

The so-called motorway team had been operating since spring the previous year, though it was autumn before the police were certain that the robberies were the work of one group. Clare had been following the team's career in the papers. Their method was two-pronged. First, they chose big houses, within five- or ten-minutes' drive at most of a motorway. Second, while the people they targeted were rich, they were not aristocrats or international businessmen – the sort of people who'd have permanent staff providing security. The team's victims were mostly celebrities, football managers, pop stars, actors, people with irregular lives who were likely to keep plenty of pricey goods about the place.

The team always struck when someone was at home, but usually when the man of the house was out. Wives were easier to intimidate into revealing hiding places when they were on their own. The team obviously had good intelligence. They probably spent a long time watching the house before deciding to strike. They left no clues that Clare had heard of, not even reliable descriptions. They wore masks and their accents varied so much that they were probably putting them on.

The waitress offered the couple a refill of coffee. Both refused.

"Is there any word on where they might be based?" Clare asked.

"Hardly. Sherlock Holmes would make a drawing of all the places they've hit and it would be a circle, with, say, Rugby in the middle of it, and that's where he'd find them. But there's no such pattern. The crimes are mainly in the Midlands, but they've gone as far north as Barnsley and as far south as Luton."

"Where do you think they're from?"

Paul shrugged.

"They're clever. It wouldn't surprise me if they were London boys. If so, they're probably known to the Met. They'll have decided that the regional police are plod and want to exploit that, commit the crimes well off their own patch."

"Makes sense," Clare said.

"They might have another car or van at the nearest services to the motorway and split up there after transferring the goods into the clean car. Maybe they've got a lock-up in Dollis Hill or Kilburn, somewhere in north London, just off the M1."

"You ought to be in CID," Clare said.

Grace shook his head.

"Promotion's too slow. I'll stick in uniform."

Paul was on the graduate fast-track. He expected to be a Chief Inspector by the time he was thirty. Clare was ambitious too, but she would never get promoted so quickly, because she had dropped out of university after four terms to join the force.

"Where to now?" Clare asked, as they got their coats.

It was hardly worth going to a pub and pushing to the front of the bar in order to get a last drink before they stopped serving. Clare considered inviting Paul back to her place. This was their third date, after all (fourth, if you counted the mess ball where he'd first made his intentions clear). But she didn't want him getting the wrong idea.

"There's a place I know two minutes away."

"Fine."

They headed into the Lace Market. Clare thought that he'd be taking her to a club: the Academy maybe, or the Monastery. She was too full to dance, but too polite to say so. As long as there was somewhere they could sit and hear themselves talk it would be OK. But Paul led her into a well-lit nook off High Pavement.

"Isn't this place a —"

"Casino, yes. Haven't you been in before?"

"No. Never."

"You'll like it."

Clare doubted that. Some people were born gamblers. She wasn't one of them. It hadn't occurred to her that Paul might be.

"Do you use this place as a drinking club?" she asked.

"Hardly. Licensing hours are the same as pubs, though it's usually easier to get served at this time. No, I thought we might check Gordon Loscoe's alibi."

Clare was relieved. Paul was like her: half his mind always on the job. Over the past three weeks, she'd been surprised by how much they had in common. They liked the same music, films, and even some of the same books. It was hard to believe that, for several months, she'd hardly noticed the Inspector as a man. His lack of height and authoritative manner stopped her taking in his quiet good looks. She was conscious only of trying to impress him as an officer. Yet now he was on her mind all the time.

The casino entrance was discreetly lit. The car-park sign was in neon, but the main entrance was a dark, wooden door, set back in what was once a lace factory. Inside, there were plush red carpets. The man at reception greeted Paul by name.

"I've a guest to sign in," Paul told him.

"Yes, sir." He opened the book. "Just put your membership number there."

"You're a member?" Clare asked, her initial worry confirmed.

"That's right. Don't look so surprised."

"You don't look the type."

"No such thing as a casino type," Paul told her. He said hello to the manager. "Gordon Loscoe in tonight?"

"Not yet. He often arrives about this time, though."

"One of your best customers?" Clare asked, with a flirtatious smile.

The manager looked back at her, poker-faced. Paul frowned. Obviously it wasn't done to talk about how much money individuals spent here.

"Remember what time Gordon left last night?" Paul asked.

"Just before one. He was here for a couple of hours. Not in any bother, is he?"

"No," Paul said. "But he's had some. I expect he'll tell you about it."

"You didn't really think that a millionaire might have robbed himself and beaten up his own wife?" Clare asked, as they climbed the stairs to the gaming area.

"I didn't. But it pays to be thorough."

They turned a corner and Clare was surprised by what she saw. The place was huge. It must extend over the whole car park as well as the offices beside and behind it. She counted a dozen roulette tables, and more where people were playing another card game. She hadn't known what to expect – women with shiny dresses showing lots of cleavage, men in smart suits with large cigars, something like that. But the place wasn't noisy. Conversations sounded concentrated, condensed. There was no music. And everyone was dressed casually. There were no trainers being worn, but plenty of jeans and open-necked shirts. Clare felt overdressed in her short black number. Paul was one of the few men wearing a tie. Only the manager wore a dinner jacket. The croupiers and floor managers wore waistcoats and black trousers, which, she noticed, had no pockets.

But the thing that most surprised her was how busy the place was. As Paul got the drinks, Clare did an approximate head count. There must be three hundred people here.

"Is it always like this?" she asked, when Paul returned with the drinks.

"Most nights, yes. The serious gamblers come in

the week, though. You tend to get more mug punters at the weekend. Amateurs out to impress."

"You come often, do you?"

"Once or twice a week, especially if I'm on nights. It's a good place to unwind. Very law-abiding, too. You never get drunks. You'd be surprised by how many coppers come here. Quite senior ones, sometimes."

"Anyone I know?"

"John Greasby's a regular. Chris Dylan comes in occasionally."

Both men were in CID.

"I always assumed that these places were for the rich, and villains."

"You get all sorts. Doubtless a few villains use the place to launder dirty money, but that can happen anywhere. What would you like to play?"

"I wouldn't."

"Oh, come on, we're here now."

Clare didn't want to explain that she had moral qualms about gambling. Paul might laugh at her.

"I'll watch you," she said. "Pick up the rules."

"All right then. Let's hope you bring me luck."

There were three games going on: stud poker, blackjack and roulette. To Clare's surprise, blackjack turned out to be the same as a game she used to play with her brother, Angelo, called pontoon, but played with money instead of matches. Paul played for ten minutes and came out even. But roulette was the fascinating game to watch. Countless chips changed hands on the spin of a wheel. Seeing her attention wander, Paul took Clare over to one of the tables. Different tables, he explained, played for different stakes.

"How do the croupiers know which chips belong to which customers?"

"Each punter has a different colour of chip. They choose the value."

Paul explained the various different kinds of bet, from gambling on a single number to betting on whether the ball would land in a red or black hole. There were seventeen of each.

"Even money," Clare said. "That's the kind of bet I understand."

"Not quite even. You'll notice that the zero hole is green. You can't bet on it. That's where the house makes its margin. One in thirty-five."

"It's not a lot, is it? Who are those people watching the croupiers?"

"Inspectors," Paul told her, with a dry laugh. "They each watch two tables, to make sure that no one's cheating, including the croupiers themselves. See that croupier over there, blowing a kiss with his lips?"

"Yes."

"He's calling an inspector over. He thinks that bloke moved a chip so that it's covering two numbers instead of one."

Sure enough, the woman came and consulted the dealer. She had a quiet word with the man, who left the table. Paul didn't miss much, Clare realized.

"The inspectors are watched by the pit bosses, who are watched by the floor manager, who is watched by the overall manager, the guy I was speaking to downstairs. Come on, let's play."

Paul, to Clare's surprise, bought £100-worth of chips.

"I usually start with fifty, but it doesn't always feel like enough."

"And when it's gone?"

"It's gone."

Paul began to play, making small bets on single numbers and losing. Then he began to put his chips down so that they covered two numbers.

"What are you doing?" Clare asked.

"Betting on both to increase my chances."

"So why didn't you do that earlier?"

"Because the odds are lower," Paul explained patiently, "sixteen to one."

For the first time he won, getting back everything he'd already lost and more. At the other end of the big room, Gordon Loscoe arrived. He looked like he'd had a few. The floor manager was making a fuss of him. Gordon was being taken over to a table at the far end of the casino that was currently unoccupied. Between spins, Clare pointed him out to Paul.

"What's happening there?"

"They keep a table clear for punters who want to play for high stakes. It'll probably just be him and the croupier. Choose a number."

Absent-mindedly, Clare picked 21.

"My birthday girl," Paul said, and put a tenner's worth of chips on it. It was her 21st on Friday, six days after Ruth's.

"No more bets."

The wheel spun. Clare found herself willing the small silver ball to find its way into the right hole. As the wheel slowed down, the ball stuttered towards the right area. It was going to fall short, Clare thought. She was wrong. Paul clapped his hands together and kissed her.

"Brilliant!"

He collected £350-worth of chips and got up.

"You're stopping?" Clare asked.

"Good gamblers always set a limit on their losses and quit while they're ahead. The other way, madness lies."

He cashed in his chips, divided the £20 notes and handed half to Clare.

"What's this for?"

"Your share of the winnings. We were a team."

"No we weren't," Clare countered. "You put up the stake."

"So what? You chose the winning number. Without that –"

Clare was tempted. She didn't have £200 to her

name at the moment. But she put on her firmest voice.

"No, Paul. Don't press it, please."

He shrugged and put the money away. On the table at the far end, Gordon Loscoe was playing, having a joke with the croupier. He ought to be at home with his wife, Clare thought, helping her get over the robbery. For some people, gambling was an obsession. As they left, Clare realized that the casino had no windows and no clocks, nothing to indicate the passing of time. It was a sealed world.

They made the short walk to the Fletchergate car park hand in hand.

"This party next week," Paul said. "Should I get Ruth a present, do you think, or just a card?"

"A card will be fine," Clare said, "but you'll be late. Her birthday's today. I mean, yesterday."

"Oh."

Clare thought for a moment, then decided to give him her prepared speech.

"Actually, I wanted to talk to you about work. When you come to the party, it's going to be obvious to everybody that we're seeing each other."

"So..." Paul said, his voice gently flirtatious.

"So, you're my boss. Things are awkward as it is, but people might accuse you of favouritism, or me of sucking up. I'm not comfortable with that."

Paul frowned. "I can't have you moved to another shift. We'd never see each other."

"I know."

"What are you suggesting then? I transfer you to South?"

"I don't want to work with Ruth. We already share a house."

"You could go on a different shift from Ruth."

"Then I'd never see *her*. She's my best friend."

"I take your point. It's a difficult one. I'll think about it."

They got into his car and made the short drive to Forest Fields.

"Do you fancy visiting the casino again some time?" Paul asked.

"I don't think so," Clare said. "I'm not that kind of girl."

"Pity."

He pulled up outside her house.

"Coming in for a nightcap?" she asked.

"Why not?"

The look on the Inspector's face told Clare that he was hoping to get lucky a second time that night. Clare wouldn't bet on it. She wasn't that kind of girl either.

3

On Sunday morning, Ben went for a run, doing a circle of the city that took him to the edge of the Maynard Estate. Thirsty, he stopped at a newsagent's to get a soft drink. He was looking in the fridge when a girl came in.

"*Lottery Winners Rolled Over*," she read out, pointing at the pile of papers, most of which led on the story of Friday night's burglary, which had happened too late to make the Saturday papers. "They used to live on this estate, didn't they, the Loscoes? I used to go to school with their Natalie. Course, she goes to some posh school now they're millionaires."

"I remember the Loscoes," Satnam agreed, selling her some gum. "They took the *News of the*

World and an *Evening Post*. Very slow to pay their paper bill."

"We had another winner on the estate Friday," the girl went on. "You know Julie Wilder? I heard down the Youth Centre that she won half a million on five numbers and a bonus ball."

"I didn't hear that," Satnam said.

But Ben knew the story. Over the weekend, it had been embellished. The amount won had gone up ten times. Julie Wilder had better watch out. Someone would be trying to burgle her.

"Yeah," the girl went on. "Dave – that's Julie's boyfriend – he's going to get a Harley-Davidson. That's what he told me."

"He'll have trouble keeping it safe on this estate," Satnam commented.

"Not Dave," the girl insisted. "He's well hard. I once saw him—"

There must have been a warning look on Satnam's face, because the girl stopped in mid-flow and turned to see Ben standing by the magazines. Everyone recognized him round here, even out of uniform. Black policemen weren't too common.

"Time I got on," the girl said, and left, sharpish.

The newsagent tried to wave away Ben's money, but he insisted on paying for his apple juice, drank it down in two gulps, then continued his run home.

Clare made 11.15 mass at the cathedral. Her mum

and dad weren't there, so she sat alone. Not that she ever felt really alone here. The same faces had surrounded her for the sixteen years she'd been coming. The priest used his sermon to go on about the Lottery. Clare was fed up of hearing about it, but there'd been something in the news this week and Father Meehan had an axe to grind.

"Today's second collection is for Christian Aid. Now I hear that some charities have had a fall in donations over recent months, as a result of people spending on the National Lottery. I've gone on about this before, but I'm going to go on about it again. People say to me, 'Well, some money from the Lottery goes to charity. It's a way of giving.' But most of it doesn't go to charity. 'Charities can apply to the Lottery for money,' they say. But some charities won't ask for Lottery money, because they believe that the Lottery is a kind of disguised taxation for the poorest in society. True, the Lottery does some good, but what it mainly does is to redistribute money from the poor to the rich. Christian Aid is one of those charities that won't take money from the Lottery, for that very reason. So please give generously."

Clare put £3 in the plate, which was more than she normally donated to the second collection. If Gary could afford to spend three quid on Lottery tickets, she could afford the same for the starving in Africa.

"House meeting," Sam said, as soon as Clare came through the front door.

"When?" Clare asked, flustered because the house was usually empty when she got in from church.

"Now. Ruth and I have been talking."

"About what?"

Clare wanted some breakfast. She hadn't had anything before going out as you weren't supposed to eat for at least an hour before taking Holy Communion.

"I noticed that Gary stayed over again last week when you were on nights."

"He didn't want to wake up the duty officer at the YMCA," Clare said, rousing herself for a row. The three women rarely had serious arguments, but sometimes bickered in a way that people sharing the same space were bound to. "Look, it's OK, isn't it?" Clare said, using her wheedling voice. "I mean, he's no trouble. He even insisted on washing the sheets."

"He's perfectly house-trained," Sam said. "I like him. In fact, we both like him. And we both think that he's the ideal person to move into the spare room."

"Oh," Clare said. "I see."

"I know we discussed this before, briefly, and you said it probably wasn't a good idea."

Clare had said this. Not because she didn't like Gary. In the past few weeks, she had become very fond of him. But not only were they on the same shift, they were currently partnered regularly. You could see too much of a person.

"The thing is," Ruth said, "he's ideal. He can cook. He's clean. He's good company. And you won't be partnering him for many more weeks. You've not been on the force long enough to be his mentor."

"I know, but—"

Ruth continued to argue.

"And if you're going to keep going out with Paul Grace, one of you is going to have to transfer to a different shift. It certainly won't be the Inspector."

Clare was very conscious of this. It was one of many good reasons for not getting involved with people at work. However, her heart, as usual, had ruled her head.

"And look at it from my point of view," Sam said. "I need the money from renting the room out. All right, there'll be another batch of students along in a few weeks, but you've got to bear in mind that a lot of people are put off by the idea of sharing a house with police officers."

"I know."

"And I must admit that, silly as it sounds, I do like having a man about the house."

The doorbell rang. Ruth answered it. "Speak of the devil," Clare heard her say. She wouldn't have been surprised if Ruth had rung and persuaded him to come over.

"Talking about me?" Gary asked, coming into the kitchen.

"Yes," Clare said, "we are."

"I didn't leave the toilet seat up last week, did I?"

All three women laughed. Clare made the decision quickly, instinctively, the way she almost always did.

"We were wondering," she said, "whether you'd like to move in with us?"

Having a baby at sixteen is no fun. Julie was doing all right at school until she got pregnant. She went back to take her exams, but, by then, her mind was off the case, and she failed them all. Brad, the baby's father, went off with someone else, and she was left at home with Mum and her younger brother. Mum wanted her out. She'd had her tubes tied after Curt and the last thing she wanted was another squawking brat about the place. But Julie, now seventeen, had nowhere else to go. And the baby was really hard work. Mum might not have been the best mother in the world, but she knew a lot more about it than Julie did. Even so, Julie hated having to rely on Mum for help.

On Friday night, it had been Mum who had knocked Curt over. Julie didn't know exactly what had happened. She'd been upstairs with Dave. But Curt had been going on about how they were going to spend the money, said something out of order, and

Mum had taken offence. Curt insisted to Julie that it was an accident. Shirley said they'd had a small fight. Julie didn't believe either of them, but she did know two things. Shirley had a violent temper on her. And you could say this about Curt: he was just as violent, but he'd never fight back against a woman.

Julie finished feeding Tammy and put her down to sleep. Curt had gone out and she hoped he'd stay out for the rest of the afternoon. Since Tammy was born, the house seemed ridiculously crowded. Julie had her name down for her own council flat, but single mothers weren't as big a priority as they used to be.

The doorbell rang. Julie left it for Mum to answer. She could do with a bit more kip herself. Dave had kept her up half the night, still spending the money for her. He'd have a brand-new motorbike. They'd rent a flat in the Victoria Centre together. Where would Tammy play? Julie asked, but Dave wasn't interested. He wanted to live in the middle of the city, so he could stagger up to bed when the clubs threw out without having to queue for a taxi, shell out the fare.

The doorbell rang again. Mum must be out, too. Someone called Julie's name. If he wasn't careful, he'd wake up the baby. She hurried downstairs. Whoever it was sounded like they'd already had a drink.

"Keep your voice down," she hissed as she opened the door. "The baby's – oh, it's you."

"Julie," slurred her father, whom she hadn't seen for seven years. "I hear you've had a bit of luck."

People in the street were staring at him. The news was still spreading, she guessed. Reluctantly, she let Dan Holt into the house.

"You're wasting your time," she said. "They haven't paid out yet. I've got to ring the local office tomorrow, to arrange to go and collect the cheque."

"But you won't forget your dear old dad when you collect, will you? Five million pounds. Twenty million split four ways. That's what they say last night's prize was."

Julie cursed. The story kept getting sillier. They'd had so many funny phone calls this morning that Mum had had to take the phone off the hook.

"I didn't win five million. I got fifty thousand on a scratch card."

"You only got fifty thou…" her father moaned. "You're lying! I heard—"

"Do you want to see the thing?"

"Damn right I do."

The scratch card had passed through so many hands that it was becoming faded. Mucky fingerprints were all over it and it had frayed at the edges. Dan Holt spat on the card and wiped clear the important figures.

"It's fifty thousand all right. A tidy enough sum."

Julie tried to take the card back off him, but he moved his hand away. Julie knew that she could afford to be patient. Her name and address were written on the back of it, in indelible ink.

"How did you find out?" she asked. "You're living in London, aren't you?"

"Watford. I read in the paper about old Gordon Loscoe being done over, so I rang up Eddie Broom."

Eddie Broom used to be her Uncle Eddie. He came round to the house occasionally, when Mum was between boyfriends. Eddie Broom, Dan Holt and Gordon Loscoe used to hang out together back in the 1980s. Mum had been out with all three of them at one time or another: Gordon before his marriage, Eddie after hers broke up.

"Eddie didn't know anything about Gordon, but he told me about your win. Seems I got the amount wrong. Still, plenty of fifty grand to go around, eh?"

"Give me that."

Her father didn't listen. Dan Holt held the card above Julie's head. Biologically, he might be her father (though he wasn't Curt's), but he had never been around for her. She owed him nothing. Dan waved the card around. Julie didn't reach for it.

"What are you?" she asked, voice heavy with sarcasm. "A child?"

"I'm only playing with you."

"You never played with me when I was a kid, did you?"

"I'll make it up to you," Dan said, his voice lacking all conviction. "Where's little Tommy? How is he?"

"It's Tammy," Julie said. "And I'm not letting you anywhere near her. As for this –"

She reached for the card and this time got it, tearing the side still further as she snatched it away from him.

"You're not getting any of it," she told her father. "What did I ever get from you? One tatty furry animal that you won at Goose Fair. It fell apart in five minutes. Oh yeah, and a pirated tape of *Snow White* one Christmas when you were trying to get Mum to sleep with you again."

"You're not being fair, Julie. I've had it hard."

"Save your stories for someone who gives a damn. I'll bet that Gordon Loscoe didn't give you a penny of his three million."

"You're wrong there."

Julie stared at him. She wasn't far wrong. She could tell that from the look on his face. So he had been round begging to Gordon Loscoe two years ago, but he hadn't even bothered to look up his daughter. That was her father all over.

"He gave me five hundred."

"Then maybe you ought to go and tap him up for more, because you're not getting anything out of me. Go on, get lost. I don't want to see you again."

To her surprise, without any further fuss, her

father got to his feet and left. The moment he'd gone, Julie burst into tears. Then Tammy started, so she had to go upstairs to feed her.

"Go on, then," Gary said. He'd been taken aback and still wasn't sure if he was doing the right thing. "We'll give it a whirl."

In turn, the three women each gave him a small hug.

"Stay for dinner to celebrate," Sam said.

"Thanks. And I don't have to give notice at the Y," Gary told her. "I could move in today."

"Fine."

"What's more, this'll put me in the clear with my parents. When I tell them that I'm moving in with three very attractive women, they'll be ecstatic."

"Oh," said Clare. "They don't know that you're…"

Gary shook his head.

"Not a clue. In fact, when I phone them, I mention you so much they're beginning to suspect that we're an item." He paused, in thought. "You don't think that this might get a bit claustrophobic – working together and living together?"

"We'll see what happens," Clare said. She didn't look too concerned. Someone knocked on the door.

"That'll be Paul," Clare told the others. "We're going rowing on the university lake."

"Getting serious?" Sam asked.

"We'll see what happens," Clare repeated, with

sly humour this time, then tossed her hair back and went to meet her Inspector boyfriend.

"I could drive you if you haven't got too much stuff," Ruth offered.

"That'd be brilliant, thanks."

"Call me when you're through."

Suddenly, Gary was alone in the kitchen. His kitchen. He'd always envisaged that his first proper place would be on his own. Or with a lover, if he was lucky. But this felt right. He rang home to say that he'd be coming to collect some more of his things soon, but wouldn't be able to make Sunday dinner.

"Three women, eh?" his dad said on the phone. "And are any of them fit?"

"They all are," Gary said, lowering his voice. "Clare especially. But they've all got boyfriends, so..."

"Boyfriends come and go," his dad said.

Tell me about it, Gary thought.

"No, you'll be in there, son. You'd make your mother's day if you brought one of those girls with you to Sunday dinner next week."

"Dad, I already said that—"

But his dad had hung up. He hated to talk for too long on the phone.

4

"They kept me in the van while they used the cards. At first, I wouldn't give them the numbers, but one of them showed me a knife and I thought, what's the point? After they'd got as much as they could, one of them hit me with something – something heavy wrapped in a plastic bag. They can't have hit me that hard. I was conscious again when they threw me out of the van, but only just. I landed awkwardly and hit my head on the side of an abandoned shopping trolley. That's the last thing I remember for a while."

Maxine Loscoe was sitting in her living room, going over her story for the umpteenth time to two CID officers, Chris Dylan and Neil Foster.

"So you don't know how much later it was when you regained consciousness?" Neil asked.

"No. I kept drifting in and out. I know that at least twice people walked by and I called for help, but they just ignored me."

They probably thought that Maxine was a prostitute, Neil guessed. Or they suspected that they were being set up for a mugging. Or they were criminals themselves. You had to be pretty hard or pretty stupid to walk across a dark, deserted inner-city car park at one in the morning, even if it was a handy short cut from Radford Road to Noel Street.

"Eventually I managed to get up. I found this shopping trolley that wasn't chained to the others, and I used it to support me as I walked to the road. Took me ages to make it to the petrol station."

"You had a lucky escape," Chris Dylan told her, in his most diplomatic voice. Actually, she'd been very unlucky. None of the motorway team's previous victims had suffered anything worse than a mild concussion from being hit on the back of the head with a gun.

"Is there anything else you can tell us about the men who took you?"

"I wish there was. But they were so frightening. They had masks on, like I said, and they talked in these phoney-sounding voices."

"They seemed to have a thorough knowledge of where all the valuables were kept around the house," Neil commented.

"They threatened to hurt Natalie if I didn't tell

them where everything was. I opened the wall safe for them. You'd have done the same in my situation."

"I'm sure I would," Neil said. "Is Natalie around?"

"In her room."

"I'd just like a quick word. See if she's remembered anything at all."

"I'll come up with you."

"No need to bother. I'm sure you have things to do."

And it was possible that Natalie would talk more easily if neither of her parents was around. She might remember suspicious people about the place, or some bloke who'd chatted her up and might have had an ulterior motive. The team had got their information about the Loscoe household from somewhere.

Natalie sat on her bed surrounded by posters of pop stars and players from the current Forest team. She was an attractive girl, but for the permanent scowl on her face. Neil made conversation by asking what school she went to.

"Hate school," she mumbled.

Neil spotted a uniform through an open wardrobe door.

"The Girls' High School, is it?"

"Yeah. Their dads are all solicitors, or doctors, or big businessmen. They're jealous, stuck-up cows, all of them. A few of them sucked up to me at first because they thought I'd give them money. They're even worse."

"Where did you go before moving here? Manvers?"

"No. Rushcliffe. I had mates there. But everyone went weird when Dad won the Lottery. Even the teachers."

"You didn't change, but they did?"

Natalie managed half a smile.

"I suppose I went a bit daft for a while, too. Nothing seemed real." She looked suspicious suddenly, as though she'd confided too much. "What did you want, anyway? You're not my shrink."

Neil was surprised. In this country, fourteen-year-old girls didn't visit psychiatrists unless they were seriously damaged – or, perhaps, seriously rich.

"Don't look at me like that," Natalie said. "I don't go any more."

Neil was beginning to wish that he had Tracey with him. She was the only woman officer on CID, and might have built a better rapport with Natalie. But Tracey and her boyfriend were on holiday in Florida until the end of the week.

"Going out with anyone, Natalie?"

"Where would I meet a bloke? It's all girls at school and Dad won't let me go back to the estate. Says I'll get mugged or something."

Neil nodded sympathetically.

"Don't you have old friends you still see?"

"There were two or three used to come over, but they've got new friends now."

"So what do you do with yourself?"

Natalie shrugged.

"I go out with me mum a lot."

They were interrupted by shouting from outside. Neil went to the window. Gordon Loscoe was arguing with a long-haired man in a wrinkled leather jacket.

"Who's that?" he asked Natalie.

"Some old friend of Dad's. Dan something. He showed up an hour ago. They've been having a drink, I think."

Neil watched as the man called Dan raised his fists to the millionaire.

"I'd better go down there."

He handed Natalie his card.

"If you think of anything that might be useful, no matter how small —"

She gave him a small grin. "Sure."

On Gordon Loscoe's vast driveway, the millionaire was shouting, "Just get lost, you old soak. That's the last time you're getting anything out of me."

The other man started swearing and Loscoe swore back. Then both of them saw Neil. He held out his warrant card so that the other man would be sure of what he was.

"Police. Is there a problem here?"

"I was just going," the old soak said.

Neil watched as he got into his car, a Ford Escort that had been tucked away under a tree, out of view. The car took four goes to start, then Gordon Loscoe went to a panel inside the house and opened the electric gates for him.

"Friend of yours?" Neil asked, when the car had gone.

"Used to be. Showed up with a sob story about how his daughter didn't want to know him. So I gave him a drink and he asks if I'll sub him a grand." He said these last words as though they were the most disgusting thing in the world.

"I suppose that – what's his name?"

"Dan Holt."

"I suppose Dan thinks that kind of amount doesn't mean much to you," Neil commented.

"No, it doesn't. But that's not the point. You can't be friends with someone one minute and begging off them the next. Last time I saw Dan was just after I won. I gave him five ton then, as a token of friendship. But I told him, don't come asking for more or we won't be mates. Do you know how many friends I've lost that way? Some people just don't listen."

Neil formulated a question carefully.

"Do you think that any of these former friends – people you've snubbed – might have broadcast details about your house and lifestyle to the men who robbed you on Friday?"

Loscoe didn't need to think for long about that one.

"It's possible. Want me to give you a list?"

In the car back to the station, Neil asked Dylan whether he'd got anything else out of Maxine Loscoe.

"She didn't hear or see anything she wasn't meant to. That team are professionals. They don't give anything away."

"If they're that professional," Neil queried, "why did they hit her so hard?"

"You heard. She banged her head against a super-market trolley."

Neil remembered, but it didn't make sense to him.

"If she was conscious enough to remember being thrown out of the van, then they didn't hit her hard enough. In each of the previous cases, they've either left the victim tied up or in a state where they won't be found for at least half an hour."

"What are you saying? Maxine's lying?"

"Confused, maybe," Neil replied. "She could have caught her head on the supermarket trolley long after being thrown out of the van. Or there's a more intriguing possibility."

"Yeah?"

"Suppose the team weren't worried about giving themselves as much time as usual for the getaway."

Dylan didn't look convinced, but he looked interested.

"Go on."

"Suppose they didn't need as much time because they're based right here, in Nottingham?"

When Ben got home from doing his early shift on Monday, there was a message on the answering machine. It was the travel agent, telling him that his tickets for Ibiza had arrived. Ben had never been on a proper beach holiday before. Charlene had always preferred more cultural pursuits, and they'd only really spent time on the beach when visiting family in Jamaica. But he was looking forward to Ibiza. So far, he and Ruth had never been alone together for more than a couple of days. They were both ready for more.

There was one thing he still had to do, however. Explain to his parents who he was going with. Mum and Dad knew that Ben wasn't seeing Charlene any more, because she hadn't been to the house for months. Even so, his mother was convinced that they'd only had a temporary spat. She was still counting on Ben marrying Charlene and their producing beautiful black grandchildren.

How to explain that he'd been seeing Ruth for nearly six months? Easier, perhaps, not to tell them about the holiday. But he was going to be gone for ten days. If he didn't contact them during that time, they'd worry. What he ought to do was to tell them about Ruth before they went away. Then Mum and Dad would have time to come to terms with the relationship before he got back.

Ben rang home and invited himself over for dinner, then decided to go into town and pick up the tickets first. If he showed them the tickets with Ruth's name on, they'd see that there was no turning back.

The Victoria Centre branch of Going Places was quiet. Only one other customer was being dealt with, an attractive-looking blonde. She was wearing sunglasses, even though it was dull out and, anyway, she was inside.

"I want a hotel where they have a baby-watching service," she was saying. Ben collected his tickets, which were already paid for. Then he waited at the exchange counter. He might as well get some currency while he was here. It would save time at the airport, and he'd probably get a better rate. The blonde girl was trying to book a last-minute family holiday in Spain. There was something familiar about her, he realized. She was from his beat.

"Deposit? I can't give you a deposit now," she was saying.

"I'm afraid that we can't confirm your booking without it," the travel agent told her.

"I should have the money on Thursday, or Friday at the latest. Will there still be places then?"

"I should think so. But this is the peak period, and a lot of places are fully booked."

"I really need to get away. Isn't there any way you can hold it for me?"

"I'm really sorry."

"OK, OK, thanks."

Julie Wilder got up to leave, then stopped at one of the racks, as if to select a brochure. In fact, Ben saw, she was crying. She took off her sunglasses, revealing a large purple bruise around her left eye. It looked fresh. Quickly, she dried her face, then put her sunglasses back on and hurried out into the street.

"Sir, can I help you? Sir?"

"Later," Ben said, as he went after her.

"Julie, wait."

Julie looked at Ben, then, not recognizing him, looked past him.

"Julie, it's Ben Shipman. From the police. I've brought Curt home a couple of times. And I was there on Friday night."

"What do you want?"

"To help."

"Get lost."

"Someone hurt you, Julie."

"So?"

Ben wondered what he was doing, getting

involved. He was off duty, after all. Julie could have already reported whoever hit her. But he doubted it.

"So, I'm worried that you might need protection. Was this to do with your win on the scratch card?"

"What if it was?"

Ben looked at his watch. He had plenty of time before the bus to Mansfield.

"Come on. Let me buy you a coffee."

To his surprise, the girl agreed. Maybe she was used to doing what men told her.

"I wish we'd never won that money," she confided in Ben, as they sat in the café by the bus station. "Not that I've got it yet. I just rang the Lottery office. It might be Friday before I get the cheque."

"Fifty thousand quid is a lot of money to wish away. What went wrong?"

"Today I saw my dad for the first time in seven years. All he wanted was money. And I split up with my boyfriend, because he was the same."

"Which of them hit you?"

Julie didn't answer. She was holding her head to one side, so that he could only see the good side of her face.

"Was it the same person who hit Curt?"

She changed the subject.

"As soon as I get the money, we're going to take a long holiday, the four of us: me, Mum, Curt and Tammy." She smiled. "Don't tell me, I know. Most people would pay *not* to go on holiday with our Curt. But he can be all right, believe it or not."

Ben smiled back. He was surprised to find himself beginning to like Julie.

"And when you come back?" he asked.

"I'm going to get a place on my own. A part-time college course, maybe. Train for some kind of job when Tammy's a bit older. After all, I can afford to pay someone to look after her now."

"Sounds like a good plan," Ben said.

Beneath the table her knee brushed his thigh. She left it there.

"Where are you going on holiday?" Julie asked, leaning forward.

Ben told her.

"Who with? Girlfriend, or wife?"

"Girlfriend."

Julie smiled, ruefully. She got up and took off her sunglasses, turning so that he could see the good side of her face properly. It was more than pretty.

"She's lucky. If you ever get tired of her…"

She left the rest of the sentence unsaid.

"Thanks for the coffee."

Julie put her sunglasses back on and left the café quickly.

5

"We've had a couple of ideas about the motor-way team," Neil told DI Greasby on Tuesday morning.

"Don't tell me, tell them."

Greasby pointed at the two suits in front of a computer screen. They were both in their early thirties, with flash ties and expensive haircuts.

"Who are they?"

"Special Task Force. Seems that, since no local force has got anywhere near the team, and the burglaries cut right across Regional Crime Squad areas, the Home Office has set up a task force to deal with them."

"But we haven't had time to –"

"Tell them that."

"Where are they based? Maybe…"

Before Neil had time to picture a glamorous secondment, Greasby squashed his fantasies.

"Forget it. They're here to go over our files, do a couple of reinterviews then head back to Solihull. The whole shebang's being run from a squad room in Brum."

As the afternoon passed, Neil went over his notes with one of the visiting officers, Phil Church, a young DC much like himself. When Neil thought he'd earned Church's respect, he brought up his theory about the gang being based in Nottingham. The Brummie DC shook his head.

"If they were based here, it's the last place they'd pull a stunt like this."

"But think about it," Neil said. "When they leave the Loscoe house and take Maxine to the supermarket, they're heading away from the motorway, towards the centre of town. That only makes sense if their hideaway is somewhere in Nottingham."

"Or if the supermarket happens to be the nearest secluded place with machines for several different kinds of cash card," Church pointed out. "Junction 26 of the M1 is only five minutes away at that time of night – seven, if they keep to the speed limit. A minute or two each way doesn't make a lot of difference. Do you know how much they got away with?"

"No."

"We've just got the figures from the banks. Eight grand in cash. Plus over a hundred grand's-worth of goods. These guys know exactly what they're playing at. And so do we."

Humiliated, Neil took off. His shift still had an hour to go, but there were no cases coming in. Everyone was dispirited about losing the Loscoe case to the Task Force. Neil was tempted to drive to Reading and see Melanie for the evening. But she was probably working at the pub where she had a summer job. Never mind. In a couple of weeks she would be returning to Nottingham, staying with him.

When he got home, Neil rang Clare. She'd been at the Loscoes' on Friday night and would want to know what had happened since. Neil missed talking over cases with Clare. Maybe she'd like to go for a drink tonight. They'd split up long enough ago to be friends again, hadn't they? Though Neil still didn't know how he would feel if she started going out with somebody new.

"Did the taxi driver remember anything?" Clare asked, when he'd brought her up to date.

"He remembered the fare. That was all. Listen. Do you fancy a drink tonight? We could—"

"I'm sorry," Clare interrupted, "I'm tied up tonight. Tomorrow, too. Maybe after work on Wednesday?"

"Play it by ear," Neil said, hiding his disappointment. "Call me then if you like."

"Time I was getting to work," Dad told Ben. He was doing a late stint on the buses. "You going to walk to the station with me, son?"

"Yes, only…" Ben paused. He'd been putting this off all afternoon. "I thought I ought to tell you both – I'm going on holiday on Sunday. Last minute thing. Ten days in Ibiza."

"On your own?" Mum asked, raising an eyebrow with just a hint of mischief.

"No. With this girl I've been seeing. Her name's Ruth."

"White girl? On the small side, with short dark hair?"

Ben was completely taken aback.

"How did you know?"

"Your sister said she'd seen you in town with a girl who looked like that. We were wondering when you were going to get round to telling us about her."

There was half a smile on his mother's face, but his father was frowning.

"I'm sorry, I—"

He was interrupted.

"Charlene knows about this, doesn't she? You broke that girl's heart, didn't you?"

Shamefaced, Ben answered his mother.

"Yes. Yes, I did."

"Well, I hope this new girl's worth it. Have a good holiday, son. You look like you need one."

Ben and his father walked to the bus station without exchanging another word.

Julie wasn't in a rush to get home, so she walked, despite the occasional drop of rain that threatened to become a fully fledged shower. She thought about the tall, handsome policeman who had bought her a coffee and wondered whether she would ever have a chance with a bloke like that. Maybe, if he didn't know her brother, or where she lived, and hadn't seen her with a black eye. Maybe, when the money came through, she would be able to buy herself some good luck.

Julie went the long way home, so that she avoided walking past Dave's place. She didn't want her other eye blackened. She called in on a couple of friends on the way. There were all sorts of stories about her going round the estate. Julie knew how stories spread, because she remembered when the Loscoes won the Lottery, and everyone turned against them. As far as Julie could recall, their only crime had been having money. Whatever they did, they were wrong: give it away and they were showing off; let someone else buy a round and they were tight bastards. You couldn't win.

Julie would have to move, too, she guessed. This afternoon, her friends had looked at her funnily when she visited. Fifty thousand wasn't so much when there were four people for it to go round, but it might as well be five million the way people on the estate saw it. It was the kind of money you only got in dreams.

But she hadn't got it yet. It might be a few days, the woman from the Lottery office said. Time to kill. With the money she'd saved by not taking the bus, Julie decided to buy herself a magazine. She liked those ones with puzzles in. They gave her something to do when she was feeding Tammy, or when she couldn't get back to sleep in the middle of the night. Stopping at the newsagent's, she found one and got out her money. The guy behind the counter wouldn't take it.

"I want a word with you."

"What about?"

"What do you think it's about?"

Julie suppressed a groan. Before she could say anything, two of the paper boys came in to collect the evening's delivery.

"Come back when it's quiet," the Asian hissed, and Julie left, quickly, with her free magazine. One more thing to worry about. And then there was Mum, at home. She'd only agreed to look after Tammy because Julie was going to the travel agent's. But she'd been gone for hours and hours. And Mum had a cleaning job at a local pub. It was a good job, which she didn't declare to the Social.

Mum would kill Julie if she'd made her late for it.

There was no sign of Mum when Julie got in. She'd left Tammy with her. Mum must have gone to work, but she'd never have left Tammy alone. Julie rushed upstairs. She'd begged Mum never to leave Tammy in the care of Curt. The men in the Wilder family couldn't be trusted for a minute.

Tammy wasn't alone. She was in the arms of her father, gurgling happily, unaware that this was the first time he had ever held her.

"Brad. What are you doing here?"

"Hi, Julie. I hear you've come into some luck."

"You really can cook," Clare told Paul Grace, finishing the last of her red onion soufflé. "That was delicious."

"Got the recipe out of *The Sunday Times*. I like cooking, when I've got time. It's relaxing. There's fruit or cheese for afters."

"No, thanks. I like to watch my figure."

Paul smiled.

"I like to watch your figure, too. Help me finish the wine, at least."

Clare had another glass of Frascati.

"I've been thinking," Paul said, "about what we were discussing on Saturday."

"You mean the shift?"

"Yes. You're right. We can't keep working together. It's messy for both of us."

"I agree. But I don't want to work on a different shift. Then we'd never see each other."

"Yeah. It's a problem. I can only see one way around it."

Clare waited, hoping it was the solution she wanted.

"You get on well with John Greasby at CID and his oppo, Chris Dylan."

"Yes."

"Their only woman officer's on holiday at the moment. John was complaining about it the other day. There's a shortage of women officers of CID calibre, that's what he reckons."

Clare said nothing. There was no shortage of calibre in the officers she met. It was just ten times harder for a woman to be accepted into CID.

"So," Paul went on, "what would you say if I arranged you a temporary transfer?"

"How temporary?"

"I can't guarantee anything. But, if things work out, say, until you've finished your probation and can apply to join CID the proper way."

"Can you get away with that?"

Paul grinned. "I have contacts in high places. But maybe it'd be a problem for you, working with your ex all the time?"

Neil. Clare wasn't going to let him get in her way.

"No. It's fine. We're friends, but there's nothing else left. He rang me today for a chat. I'm sure he'd be happy to work with me again."

"That's sorted then. I'll ring John tomorrow."

Clare gave him a big, wet kiss.

"You're wonderful, you know that?"

"I do my best."

They sank into his settee together.

"I'm crazy about you," Paul whispered, as he caressed her. "Why don't you stay the night?"

"I hope you haven't been trying to bribe me to sleep with you," Clare teased him.

"Of course not."

"Good. Because you're just going to have to wait until I'm really sure." Paul moaned, as though in pain. Clare felt sorry for him. If he'd begged a little more, maybe she'd have given in. Paul didn't know how tempted she was. But he took her at her word and called a taxi to take her home when she asked him to.

"I love you, Julie. I've always loved you."

"Then why did you leave?"

Brad looked her straight in the eyes. He had blue eyes and long, curly hair that was almost as fair as her own. She'd been the envy of every girl in her year when she went out with him.

"Because I freaked. I was seventeen. I wasn't ready to be a father."

"And I was only fifteen. How do you think I felt?"

"But you seemed to take it in your stride. There

are lots of girls that age, believe me, who want nothing more than to have a baby. That's why I never took chances. I always wore a condom." He had the good grace to look embarrassed, then added, "except that one time."

"Once was enough."

She should have taken the pill as well. She knew that. Mum told her to, when she cottoned on that Julie and Brad were having sex. Belt and braces, she said. But Julie was too embarrassed to go to the clinic.

"Isn't she beautiful?"

Julie nodded slowly.

"She's got your eyes." Her ex-boyfriend made little cooing noises to his daughter.

"What are you doing here, Brad? Why did you come?"

"Everyone's been talking about you. I suddenly realized how much I missed you, how crazy it was that I'd never seen my daughter. So I walked out of college and came over here. What happened to your eye?"

"My boyfriend and I broke up."

"Because he hit you?"

"He hit me when I told him that I wasn't giving him the money to buy a motorbike. Then I broke up with him."

"Oh, Julie."

Brad put down the baby and hugged her. He felt

good. He smelt good. Old feelings came flooding back. Brad was the only boy she'd ever really been in love with. So many nights she'd spent dreaming of a reunion like this. But why did it have to be now?

"You still look great."

"Sure," Julie said, sarcastically.

Brad wasn't his real name. That was Geoffrey, or something equally square. He'd changed it when he was thirteen, named himself after an American actor, one who, as far as Julie was concerned, couldn't act. Which was appropriate, actually, because Brad wasn't too good an actor, either. Though when you were as good-looking as he was, you could always find a string of pretty girls willing to believe your romantic lies.

"So what are you going to do with the money?"

How much did he think she'd won? Fifty thousand? Five hundred thousand? Five million? How much had he decided to ask for?

"I'm thinking of giving it to charity," she said. "So if you can think of any good causes, send me a letter. But now I'm going to feed Tammy, and I don't want you watching."

"But I'm her father," Brad protested, jokily.

"Your name isn't on the birth certificate," Julie told him. "When the Child Support Agency asked, I said I didn't know who the father was. Course, if you really want to be the father, you could take a blood test. You could see Tammy, say, alternate weekends. Oh, yes, and pay child support for the next fifteen years. Do you know how much it costs to bring up a child? A lot more than I won on the Lottery. Have you got any idea how much I've given up to look after Tammy? I could have had an abortion, like you wanted, but I didn't."

"That was your choice," Brad argued, the fake tenderness gone from his voice.

"And I don't regret it. What I do regret is ever believing in you. But I don't any more. So go. Now."

Brad gave her a look of utter contempt. There was a familiar banging from below: Curt charging up the stairs. He thrust open the door without knocking.

"What's he doing here?"

Brad looked at Curt. The boy had grown since Brad had seen him last. They were roughly the same size, but Julie had no doubts: Curt could take him. Brad looked like he knew it, too.

"He's just going," Julie said.

"Good."

When the front door slammed, Tammy began to cry and Julie fed her.

"How's your eye?" Curt asked.

"A bit sore. I'll put some more cream on when I've finished doing this."

"Let me do it."

With surprising gentleness, Curt massaged ointment into her bruised skin.

"How was school today?" she asked him.

The unit wasn't really a school, but they always called it that.

"Didn't go. I was looking for that Dave."

"I told you not to."

"He's cleared right off, anyway. But when I find him –"

"I said forget it," Julie said, though, in a way, she was touched by her brother's loyalty. "I'm well rid."

"You didn't tell him, did you?"

Julie wasn't sure if Curt meant Brad or Dave, but the answer was the same in either case.

"No, of course not."

"You think he worked it out?"

"Dave? I doubt it. He's a bit thick, when it comes down to it. I don't know what I saw in him, I really don't."

She paused, then added:

"But there is someone we need to watch out for."

Curt's face became hard, wary.

"Who?"

6

The phone rang at nine, when Clare was still in bed.

"Wake you up, did I?"

She recognized the voice of DI Greasby.

"I'm not on duty until tomorrow," Clare explained.

"You are now," Greasby told her. "Paul Grace rang me five minutes ago, and asked me to invent a job for you."

"Oh. Right."

"So, officially, you're acting as our liaison with Solihull over this motorway gang."

"Wow!" Clare said.

"Don't get excited. It's a rubbish job – a one-way street. They think we're plod, don't want anything to do with us. But unofficially, I do need a female officer to be available when a bloke isn't appropriate. We'll revise your role when Tracey gets back."

"Fine. Thank you."

"Don't thank me, thank your Inspector. And get over here."

"I'm on my way."

Clare dressed in the smartest clean clothes that she could find, then borrowed Ruth's car to get to the station. The first person she saw when she walked through the door was Neil.

"What are you doing here?" he asked.

"Reminding you about the party on Saturday. You're coming, aren't you?"

"Course I am."

"Bringing Melanie?"

"No. She's coming back to Nottingham the week-end after. Needs to earn as much money as possible before then. I'll come on my own, or I might meet up with Jan first. I don't suppose she'll be bringing Kevin along. He hates police dos."

"It's not a police do!" Clare protested, though, now she thought about it, practically everyone who was coming was in the job. "But you won't get Jan. She and Kevin flew to Tenerife on Sunday. She's not back for a fortnight." Which, now she came to think of it, meant that her shift was two down and had no female officers. But that wasn't her problem. It was Paul's.

"What are you doing dressed like that?" Neil asked.

She was wearing a short black skirt and a light blue blazer, with a white blouse beneath.

"Is that a compliment or an insult?"

When Neil didn't reply, she continued. "I'm filling in for Tracey, and doing some liaison with the Solihull Task Force, which none of you lot want to do, or so I'm told."

Neil raised both eyebrows, but said nothing. His pager went off. DI Greasby waved Clare into his office.

"Not a lot for you to do today, I'm afraid."

Then why bring me in on my rest day? Clare wondered, but didn't ask.

"Acquaint yourself with the Loscoe burglary file. If any new intelligence comes in, collate it and type it on to the computer."

"Then fax it to Solihull?"

"Only if they ask for it," Greasby said. "Brummie boys haven't decided that the Loscoe burglary is one of theirs yet."

"Why not?"

"Seems they're working on the theory that a couple of the ten may be copy-cat cases."

"How would they prove that?" Clare asked.

"Evidently in eight of the nine other cases, the gang used guns. Maxine and Natalie Loscoe only mentioned knives."

"Which doesn't mean that they weren't carrying guns."

"I know, but if the task force do manage to dump the Loscoes, they'll throw the mess back at us, so make sure that the files are up to date. And while you haven't anything important to do, make some coffee, would you?"

Clare had been here before, playing the office dogsbody. She knew better than to resist.

"Of course," she said.

Clare put some coffee in a filter, filled the cavity with water, and turned the machine on. Then she looked up the Loscoe files on the computer. They were full of typing errors and there were endless omissions.

"This is a mess," she said to Neil.

"New system. No one's quite used to it yet."

There was a task for her here, Clare realized. If she became proficient on the latest operating system, she could make herself indispensable. Computing wasn't what she'd come into the police force to do. It was, however, something she was good at. She looked through the manual, remembering how she'd helped her younger brother, Angelo, when he got his first computer. It was less than a year, though, before he was teaching her.

Clare had the main points of the system sussed within fifteen minutes. She and Neil finished their coffee together.

"Time I was going," Neil said, draining his mug.

"Anything interesting?"

"A newsagent – he's on your beat, actually – got assaulted this morning when he was opening up. He didn't want to report it, wouldn't say why. Family feud maybe, or some kind of Asian gang thing. But someone called it in and the uniforms have passed it over to us. Come if you like. Might be worth a couple of us asking around the Maynard Estate, see if anyone saw anything."

Clare sighed.

"I thought I was finally shot of the Maynard Estate."

"Still your patch, I'm afraid."

This CID unit covered both East, where Clare worked, and South, which was Ruth's beat.

"OK," Clare said. "I'm up for it."

"I'll clear it with the boss."

They arrived at the newagent's just before eleven, a quiet time of day. The owner, Satnam Singh, had his arm in a sling, but was still working. Neil flashed his warrant card at him.

"I told the men earlier. I have nothing to say. Nothing happened."

"Fair enough," Neil said. "Might as well do one of these while I'm here." He took a National Lottery slip and began to fill in some numbers.

"Isn't this where Gordon Loscoe bought his winning ticket?" Neil asked, handing the form to the newsagent, who put it through the machine.

"No. He bought it from the post office, I think."

"Pity. Selling a winner must boost your sales."

Satnam didn't seem enthusiastic.

"It's good for business, yes."

"See anything of the Loscoes since they moved to greener pastures?"

"Only one of them. The girl, what's she called?"

"Natalie."

"Natalie used to come back, visit friends. They'd come in here. But not for a long time."

"How do people feel about the Loscoes round here?" Clare asked.

"They're not what you would call popular. Why are you asking me this? You think someone from here robbed them? Is that why you've come?"

"No," Neil said, "we've come because somebody mugged you. But since you won't talk to us about that, we're asking you about the Loscoes to pass the time. Would Gordon Loscoe have any former friends who might feel particularly aggrieved about him leaving them behind?"

The newsagent thought for a moment. Clare could see him weighing up the situation. Essentially, Neil had offered him a deal: give us some dirt on Loscoe and we won't press you about what happened this morning. Clare didn't like it.

"Gordon had a lot of – what would you call them? – drinking buddies," Satnam replied, eventually. "The only person I'd see him on the street with was called Eddie. Eddie didn't seem to have a job.

Sometimes he helped Gordon restore cars, maybe. They were often together. But I don't think Eddie lives around here any more."

"OK," Neil said. "Thanks for your help. And if you change your mind…"

"Thank you."

"I'll be back for my winnings," Neil said on his way out.

"I've never known you do the Lottery before," Clare said, as they returned to the car.

"I do it now and then. It's for a good cause, isn't it?"

"Only a quarter of the ticket cost. You'd do better buying a copy of *The Big Issue* or spending money in an Oxfam shop."

"You're very moral today," Neil said. "It's a laugh, that's all. And it gave me a few seconds to think about how to deal with Satnam."

"I thought you were going to get the names and addresses of his paper boys and girls," Clare commented. "See if any of them got there early, saw something."

"I decided to forget it," Neil said. "There's no crime to investigate."

"How do you mean?"

"Before we saw Satnam, I thought maybe somebody had scared him off. But he wasn't intimidated. He had that 'I'm going to sort it out myself' look."

"And you're going to let him sort it out, whatever

it is?"

"Sure," Neil said. "After all, think about it: how would we stop him?"

"I don't like it when people take the law into their own hands."

"Not even when it's someone like Roy Tate?"

Tate was a police officer who had badly beaten up a youth who raped his granddaughter.

"Especially when it's a police officer," Clare replied. "Have they decided if Roy's going to be prosecuted?"

"Word is that the Crown Prosecution Service declined to press charges. The victim could bring a private prosecution, but it's unlikely – he left the area as soon as he'd discharged himself from hospital. Roy still has to retire, of course, but he gets to keep his pension."

"Good for him," Clare said.

She was relieved for Roy but worried about the message being sent out by the CPS: private justice was acceptable. She didn't know what kind of vendetta Satnam Singh was involved in. Maybe Neil was right: better not to waste police time with it. But what happened if someone got badly injured, or worse, and the police had ducked out of investigating? Whose responsibility was it then?

"Why does it take so long?" Curt asked, still aggravated because the prize cheque wouldn't be presented until Thursday, or maybe even Friday.

"They said something about having to verify it."

"Do you think they'll…?"

"How should I know?" Julie asked.

"What if they go to Batman?"

This was what all the local kids called the newsagent.

"Maybe I should go to see him. Offer to…"

"No. No one outside the family. We agreed."

"Yeah, but he *knows*."

"I know he knows," Curt said. "But think. He can't prove it. And, if he tells, no one on this estate'll buy a Lottery ticket from his shop again. And he'll need good medical insurance. Todd and I told him that this morning."

Todd was a hard kid from the referral unit who Curt went around with sometimes.

"Oh, God," Julie said. "You didn't do anything to him, did you?"

"Not much. Enough."

Julie was angry.

"You know what'll happen if you get caught again – you'll be inside. Glen Parva. And we might lose the money, too. It's not worth it. Look, I'll go and see Satnam, offer him a couple of grand."

"Over my dead body," Curt warned.

Julie left it. Why were all the men she knew hell bent on violence? She thanked the heavens that her baby was a girl.

7

Ben began his afternoon shift on Wednesday feeling positive. It was a three-day week. This time on Sunday he'd be at Birmingham airport, boarding.

The parade room was unusually quiet. Jan was on holiday. Tim Cooper was off sick, again. But where was Clare?

"I'm coming with you today," Paul Grace told Ben. "We're three short."

The morning shift briefed the afternoon shift on the day's events. Nothing out of the ordinary. Gary and John were sent out walking on the Maynard Estate. Ben waited while the Inspector finished some paperwork, then joined him in a car.

"I hope Clare's better in time for her birthday on Friday," Ben commented.

He knew that Paul Grace was seeing Clare, had been for two or three weeks. The word was right around the shift now, probably all over the station.

"Clare isn't ill," Grace told him. "I've transferred her temporarily. In fact, I've just been arranging a replacement for her."

"I see."

"I'm glad we've got this chance to work together," Grace continued. "There's something I wanted to discuss with you."

"Sir?"

"Your probation ends this week. If I know you, Ben, you're already thinking about studying for your sergeant's exams."

"I've bought a couple of books," Ben admitted, as they drove out towards Hyson Green.

"I want you to think about becoming a mentor."

A mentor, or tutor officer, was responsible for guiding a probationer through the active service part of training.

"Really?"

Grace nodded.

"I know that your own experience of being mentored wasn't entirely successful."

This was true. Ben had fallen out with Jan Hunt when she was his tutor officer. In fact, Ben hadn't had a mentor at all since Neil transferred to CID.

"I had a mixed experience," Ben admitted.

"Which makes you keen to do better for whoever

you take under your wing."

"Yes, sir. Who did you have in mind? Someone new?"

Grace shook his head.

"I want you to tutor Gary."

"Really? You know that—"

"He shares a house with Clare and Ruth? Yes, of course I know. It makes no difference to anything."

There was a pregnant pause as they drove past the Forest. Grace went on.

"You also know that Gary's homosexual."

"Yes."

Gary wasn't out, but Ruth had told Ben that he was gay.

"Does that make a difference to you?" the Inspector asked.

Ben considered. Homosexuality made him uncomfortable, there was no denying that. But he liked Gary.

"I don't have a problem with it," Ben said, diplomatically.

"Good. Because most straight officers do, whether they admit it or not. Nevertheless, it's as important to have gay officers as it is to have black ones."

"Why?" Ben asked, then bit his lip, because he hadn't meant to say this aloud.

"Because the police have to represent every section of the community. Some forces have even advertised for recruits in the gay press."

"Really?"

"Do you know how many out gay coppers there are in Notts?" Grace asked.

"I have no idea. I only know of one."

"Exactly. We need more. Gary's not out yet, but several people have heard about him. Word's bound to get around. There'll be all kinds of jibes. Some of those will be aimed at you, too. Think you can handle it?"

"Yes, sir."

"Good. And, congratulations. You passed your probation with flying colours."

"Hold on, DC Coppola's dealing with that," Dylan said, gesturing Clare to pick up her line.

Clare flushed with pride. She wasn't really a DC, being only on temporary assignment, but she was part of the team now, so was referred to as a detective, as a courtesy. The caller was from the company that insured Gordon Loscoe. Clare gave the loss adjuster the crime number she wanted. The adjuster wanted to know if the police thought the claim was genuine.

"We've had nothing to indicate otherwise," Clare said.

"And was it – you know – the motorway team?"

"You'd have to check with the task force in Solihull on that," Clare said.

There was still the matter of whether the gang ever used knives to be resolved, but Clare couldn't give the loss adjuster such sensitive information. The police always described the burglars to the media as "armed", giving only vague details, making it harder for copycats to turn the team's methods into a boom industry.

"It's just that I was involved when the team did –" The loss adjuster mentioned the name of a famous football manager who had been done over the year before. "Professional interest, you could say. Thanks anyway."

"Hold on."

The adjuster was about to ring off, but Clare kept her on the line. Maybe she could learn something that Solihull weren't telling her.

"Does it look like the same team from your point of view?" she asked.

"The kinds of things they took are very similar – cash cards, jewellery, expensive knick-knacks. Nothing too bulky. Nothing that's difficult to sell on. What's different from our point of view is that a lot of the stuff they stole was bought very recently."

"Gordon only won the Lottery a couple of years ago," Clare pointed out.

"No. I mean, really recently, in July and August. It's probably a sign that the Loscoes are spending all the time, but we always have to be on the look out for inflated claims."

"I'd have thought that the Loscoes didn't need to rip you off," Clare commented.

"We reckon that between one in two and one in three claims are inflated," the adjuster told her. "And some of the biggest cheats are the wealthy ones. That's how they hang on to their money. But proving it…"

Clare logged the call on the computer, then trawled her memory. When Neil was questioning Satnam the day before, he came up with a name: Eddie. No surname. She typed Gordon Loscoe's name into the computer and ran a Police National Computer check on him. You never knew what that would turn up. Gordon had a string of minor convictions, all of them spent: theft, obtaining money by false pretences, nothing quite serious enough to merit a prison term.

You could say that Loscoe's convictions were an inevitable consequence of his working on the fringes of the used-car trade. One in three second-hand cars had a suspect history. Cars were written off, sold for spare parts, and turned up again, restored by people like Gordon Loscoe. Often the new owners had no idea that their pristine-looking motor had been in a bad accident.

But Clare wasn't especially interested in Loscoe. She was interested in his associates, the people charged with him. If she was lucky… There it was, eight years ago. Loscoe had been charged with conspiracy to defraud. His co-defendant was one Edward Broom. Loscoe got a big fine. Broom did six months. Clare typed him into the computer.

Eddie Broom's last known address appeared on the computer screen. It was on the Maynard Estate. Clare double-checked the address with, first, the phone book and then the electoral register. The most recent appearance of his name was three years ago. Eddie had been done for speeding three times in the past two years, on the M1, M69 and M6, each time giving the old address. Another time and he'd lose his licence. Clare needed an excuse to question Broom. She could probably do him for giving a fake address. It wouldn't come to court. He'd argue that it was an oversight: he hadn't got round to getting the address on his licence changed. It didn't matter. She'd get to see him. But she had to find him first.

Clare had a thought. She clicked on the file that showed the location and timing of each of the motorway gang's jobs. While she was printing this information off, she went down to Ruth's car, which she was borrowing, and got out the big mapbook. Back in the office, she took the dates of Eddie Broom's driving offences and looked up the robberies that occurred nearest to them. There was one in Watford, another in Coventry. A third, the furthest afield, took place in Preston. Each robbery happened during the month after Eddie was caught speeding on the adjoining motorway. It was tenuous, but just suppose that Eddie Broom was working surveillance for the motorway team?

Suppose he had decided to get his own back on his old pal Gordon by setting him up?

Calmly, Clare typed out a report, showing what she'd found. It took an hour, interrupted only by her making coffee for the other officers. She would send it to Solihull, after she'd shown it to Neil. Clare knew what Solihull would say: the links she'd found proved nothing. But, taking no chances, they would interview Eddie, or authorize Nottingham to do so, when and if they found him.

"Where's Curt?" Mum asked Julie when *Central News* had finished. "He should be back by now."

Today was dole day. Curt had been sent out to buy three lots of fish and chips. Julie checked her watch.

"He's been gone too long," she agreed.

"You'd better check. I can't go outdoors like this."

Mum was in her dressing gown. She'd just had a bath, because she was meeting a new boyfriend later that night.

"Here," Julie said, handing her mother the baby.

But there was no need. The front door opened, slowly.

"About bloody time," Mum said.

Julie knew that something was wrong before she saw Curt. There was no fish-and-chip smell. Curt limped in, dripping blood. His face had been smashed to a pulp. His clothes were torn, and his left arm hung lifelessly at his side.

"Call an ambulance," Julie said.

"No," Curt insisted. "I'm all right."

"Like hell you are. What happened?"

"Mates of Satnam's. They jumped me."

The phone rang. Julie answered it. She recognized the voice on the other end.

"Your little brother made it home, then."

"What do you want?"

"I told you to come and talk to me. Instead you sent that little thug and his mate to beat me up. If you'd come and talked, you'd have saved him a lot of pain and yourself quite a bit of money."

"What are you going on about?" Julie asked, though she had a good idea what he was going to say next.

"If you'd seen me when I wanted you to, I was only going to ask for two thousand. Now I want ten."

"You're not—"

"Any argument and it goes up to twenty. Think about it. You and Curt still get forty thousand. Or you don't pay me and you get nothing at all."

"It doesn't work like that," Julie argued. "I signed the ticket."

"Ten thousand, as soon as the cheque clears. In cash. Either you agree or I call—"

Julie had no choice. She gave in.

"I agree."

"Good. And take a look at what happened to your brother. Imagine what the same blokes could do to little Tammy. Because that's what'll happen if you let me down."

Satnam hung up. Julie burst into tears.

"What is it?" Mum said. "Who was that?"

Julie told her.

"He threatened Tammy. And look what he did to Curt."

Her brother was still bleeding all over the vinyl sofa while Mum tried to bandage his torn shoulder.

"That's it," Julie said. "I've had enough. I'm calling the police."

"No police," Curt managed to splutter. "We'd lose all the money."

"You're not talking sense," Mum told Julie. "We don't need any police. I'll sort this out. I'll call Eddie."

8

"Do you see what I see?" Gary asked John Farraday.

John looked at the mess on the pavement.

"Someone's spilt their chips and tomato ketchup?"

"That's a lot of chips," Gary said. "But I don't think it's tomato ketchup."

John leant down to get a closer look.

"You're right. Anyway, now I come to think of it, the chippy down the road gives you ketchup in those little sachets. They make you pay for it."

"Times are tight," Gary commented. "You know, this is a lot of blood."

A couple of lads were walking towards them.

"Did you see what happened here?" Gary called to one of them.

"Not me," the youth said, and kept walking.

On the Maynard Estate, getting people under thirty to talk to the police was an uphill task. Even with those over thirty, your chances were never better than even.

"We don't need a witness," John Farraday said.

"What do you mean?"

John pointed along Vernon Gapper Way.

"Doesn't take a tracker dog to follow that trail."

The crimson drops led straight to the home of Shirley Wilder.

Clare cooked her famous cannelloni for dinner.

"Fancy joining us for a girls' night out?" Ruth asked Sam.

Ben and Paul Grace were working until 10pm, while Ruth was on earlies and Clare was doing a nine to five.

"Can't," Sam said. "I'm going to Steve's play."

"Aren't we invited?" Clare asked petulantly.

"Anyone can buy a ticket," Sam said. "It's on for two nights."

"Tell us if it's any good," Ruth said. "We'll go tomorrow."

"You can manage the short walk to the Arts and Crafts Centre, can you?" Sam asked, playfully, then added: "Don't worry about it. Steve won't be expecting either of you two."

Clare felt vaguely hurt. It was true, she had

arrested Steve once, but he had also helped the police on a couple of occasions. As far as she was concerned, the slate was clean between them. Maybe she even owed him a favour, like going to see his first performance in a play.

"Actually," Ruth said, "there was something I've been meaning to ask you."

"Don't tell me," Sam said, getting out a pocket mirror and freshening up her face. "Am I bringing Steve on Saturday?"

"That was it."

"What's the problem?" Clare said, seeing, immediately, that there was one. Would officers like Paul, or Chris Dylan, be comfortable letting their hair down when there was a convicted burglar in their midst?

"Don't worry," Sam replied. "Steve wouldn't come even if I dragged him. A party full of police officers isn't exactly my idea of fun, but Steve would run a mile. Anyway, I'm not sure if Steve and I will still be an item by Saturday."

"You think he's going to drop you?" Ruth asked, her voice concerned.

"The other way round, thank you very much. Drop them before they drop you – that's always been my style."

"What's wrong with him?" Clare wanted to know.

"Nothing," Sam replied, "except that I'm too old for him and he's bound to meet someone else. All our relationship has ever been good for is sex."

"That's a lot better than nothing," Ruth said.

"It's great for a few weeks, but then it starts to fizzle out. That's what happened the first time I went with him and it'll happen again. So I've decided to quit while there's still a spark. I've been leaving it until the play's over. Talking of which … time I was going."

"Poor Steve," Clare said, when Sam was gone.

Ruth laughed.

"Poor Steve nothing. He's using Sam because she happens to live two streets away. She's convenient. With looks like his he can get someone else any time he wants, if he can be bothered."

"There's more to them than that," Clare said. "I think he needs her, and she kind of needs him, but neither of them is willing to admit it."

"Believe me," Ruth said, "it's only about sex. Talking of which, are you and the Inspector doing it yet?"

"*Please!*" Clare said. "You've got this really … tactless way of leaping into things. It's less than a month since we started seeing each other."

"Let me tell you something about the real world," Ruth offered. "Most people wait less than a week."

"I'm not most people. You know I never slept with Neil, not once."

"I know," Ruth said. "You had to wait until you were sure that you were in love with him. Good old patient Neil. He waited and waited and in the end all he got was dumped."

"That's not fair."

"The way it looks to me is that you weren't fair with him. But I can't see the Inspector being quite so patient."

"No," Clare admitted. "Neither can I."

"So," Ruth pressed, "are you falling in love with him?"

"What's going on here?" The new young policeman asked.

"Nothing," Shirley Wilder protested.

"Nothing?" the older policeman mocked. "There's a trail of blood leading to your door."

"Our Curt had a nosebleed."

"So bad that he dropped the entire family dinner? Pull the other one."

"Would you mind if we came in?" the younger one asked. "Just to make sure that Curt's all right."

"You've never been bothered about me before," Curt called from the sofa. Then, somehow, the young one got into the room. He was quite tasty, when you took a proper look at him, if a little on the pudgy side.

"What happened, Curt?" he asked.

"Nothing."

"Come on."

"I walked into a lamppost."

"The fish and chips weren't scattered anywhere near a lamppost," the older one said, Shirley having let him in, too. "You look like you need a hospital. I'll call an ambulance."

"No!" Shirley protested. "I can get him to Casualty myself."

"How? You don't have a car, and no taxi's going to take him when he's bleeding like that."

"Tell us what happened, Curt."

"No. We'll sort it out ourselves."

"You're the victim of a serious assault."

A new voice joined the fray.

"You heard the lad."

Everyone looked round. Uncle Eddie had walked in through the open door. He'd put on a little weight, but his expensive clothes masked it well. His confidence sounded less put on than it used to. He must be going up in the world.

"Who are you, sir?" the older officer asked.

"A family friend. Shirley here called me to take Curt to Casualty, which is what I'm going to do once you're gone and we've got him cleaned up. All right?"

"For now," the young one said. "But we can't leave it like this. He'll have to tell us what happened."

"Then come back in a couple of days. Curt's in shock. Anyone can see that." The officers looked at each other. Uncle Eddie was convincing – he ought to be, he was a complete con man, as Shirley never tired of telling Julie after Eddie walked out on her. But they both had a soft spot for him.

"We'll pass this on to CID," the older one said. "Oh, and before we go, can I have your name, sir?"

"Certainly. It's Broom. Eddie Broom."

"All right. Thank you."

When they were gone, Julie told him what had happened.

"You should have called me straight away," he said, when she'd finished. "I'd have helped out. That's what friends are for, eh, chuck?"

He pinched Julie's cheek, the way he used to when she was a child.

"All our friends want is a cut of the money," she pointed out.

"That I can believe. Taking off on holiday, that's a sensible idea. Maybe I'll come along – when were you planning on going?"

"Sunday," Shirley said. "But—"

"Don't worry, duck. I'll pay me own way. I'm loaded, you know that."

Eddie always claimed to be loaded. Julie had no way of telling whether it was the truth.

"I suppose we'd better take Curt to Casualty. Don't want to be permanently scarred, do you, Curt? Get us an old sheet or something, Shirley love. I don't want his blood all over the back seat of my Merc."

He bundled Curt into the car, taking Shirley with him. Eddie would use any excuse to work the old charm on her.

"If Jeff calls," Mum whispered to Julie, "tell him Curt had an accident. I'll make it up to him another time."

"And if that newsagent calls again," Eddie said, making it clear that he'd heard, "make it sound like nothing's changed. Be scared. All right?"

"All right."

Julie *was* scared. All she wanted to do was get out of the house, take Tammy and go somewhere else, anywhere else, tonight. She had no money and nowhere to go, however. But at least now she had Eddie Broom.

"Maybe I *am* falling in love," Clare replied. "And it scares me."

"Why?"

Clare wondered whether to confide in Ruth. She was her best friend. There had never been anyone closer. But everyone had secrets. Ruth rarely talked about her old life, in Halifax. Clare gathered it had often been unhappy. As far as Ruth was concerned, Clare's history started with her brother Angelo being killed, and her meeting Neil, almost exactly two years ago.

"Is it to do with sex?" Ruth asked gently. "Are you scared of it?"

"Course not," Clare said, then hesitated. "But I am wary."

"Because of your religion?"

Clare smiled and shook her head.

"I'm not so very religious. And I'm not a virgin."

"What? I thought—"

"I know what you thought. And, as for Neil, I let him think that."

"I don't understand," Ruth said.

"I wouldn't make love with Neil until I was *in love* with him. But I never fell in love. Or maybe I wouldn't let myself."

"Why?"

"Because, both the times that I let it happen before, I got hurt really badly."

Clare put her head in her hands, lost in thought. Ruth waited a while, then prompted her.

"You've had two lovers."

"Yes," Clare said, deciding that she might as well tell Ruth about it.

"The first was called Max. My first proper boy-friend. He was in the year above me at sixth-form college. He bowled me over. At school, I'd never taken any of the boys seriously. They'd ask me out, but it was like I'd grown up with them and they were family. As for the Italian boys I met, we never clicked at all. But Max was from another world. He looked like a Greek god. His parents had money. He drove a nice car. He told me he loved me. It was the

93

old cliché. He swept me off my feet. I waited a whole week before having sex with him. All I remember is that it hurt. The next week I found out that he was seeing at least two other girls at the same time."

"Ugh."

"So I dumped him. I still see him around occasionally. I think he works for his dad's company as a rep, something like that."

"And do you feel anything?"

"Nothing at all," Clare said, with a wry smile. "From what I've seen, he still goes out with girls the age I was then."

"Some men never grow up," Ruth said. "So when did you meet the other guy?"

"I dated boys after Max, but I never went all the way. Then, in my second term at university, I fell for someone else. Karl. He looked a bit like Steve Garrett, actually. Tall, long hair, very good-looking, liked all kinds of music and took all kinds of drugs."

Ruth raised an eyebrow.

"He was in the year above me, on the same course: architecture. I was always seeing him around. He kind of pursued me in my first term, but I was sort of seeing someone else and, anyway, he scared me a little. Next to him, I felt ordinary, strait-laced. Then I came home for Christmas and Nottingham seemed so dull after Manchester. I was bored senseless. I was ready for a romance. On my first day back at university I bumped into Karl and he asked me out. I said yes, but I tried not to jump straight in. After a couple of weeks I couldn't resist. We had a wild time. I hardly did any work that term."

"You did drugs?" Ruth asked.

"I dabbled a bit," Clare said. "But sex was like a drug for me. I'd never realized how wonderful it could be. I spent the entire spring term on a permanent high."

"Then what happened?"

"I practically moved in with Karl that term, but I had to go home at Easter because the hall of residence would be closed, and I couldn't explain to Mum and Dad that I was staying with my boyfriend. While I was in Nottingham, he hardly called. I thought that was because he wasn't very good on the phone. But when I got back for the summer term, he'd changed."

"Just like that?"

"He told me we'd had a great time but, as he thought about it, he'd realized that I was too straight for him. Next thing I knew he was going out with a girl who had matted hair, a giant-sized nose ring and every single item of her clothing tie-dyed."

"Ouch."

"It was even worse than with Max. Karl and I were together three months. I was having daydreams of bearing his children. I more or less swore off men after that. Then Angelo died, and I couldn't concentrate on anything any more. I dropped out. The rest you know."

Ruth was silent for a while.

"Did you tell Neil any of this?" she asked, eventually.

"Only obliquely. I don't exactly enjoy going over my past humiliations. And it was a kindness, too. He assumed that I was a virgin. If he'd known otherwise, he might have felt humiliated, or cheated, I don't know. But I'd promised myself that I wouldn't sleep with anyone else unless I was really, really sure that we were in love with each other. I wanted true love, not the kind of infatuation I felt with Max and Karl. But I never even felt infatuated with Neil."

"He loved you."

"I know. And I loved him, but like a brother. Not like…"

"And Paul Grace?"

Clare hesitated.

"I'm not sure how I feel. I knew him for months before even realizing that I fancied him. He's not tall, or muscular, and he's really bossy."

"A bit like you."

Clare laughed.

"And I want him so much," she went on. "But *love*. I don't know what it means any more. Paul doesn't talk about it. Sometimes I think that there are two kinds of people in the world – the ones who believe in love and the ones who don't. Maybe all that true love stuff's for adolescents."

"And Paul's a grown-up."

"He certainly is."

Clare looked straight into Ruth's eyes.

"What do you think? Do you believe that for every woman, there's one true love?"

"Yes," Ruth replied. "Yes. I know it's silly but, yes, I do."

Meaning Ben. Clare smiled encouragingly.

"And you?" Ruth asked her.

Clare thought for a moment, but it wasn't any clearer.

"I wish I knew," she said. "I wish I knew."

9

Julie woke early and fed Tammy, then waited for the post. The Lottery office had said they'd ring, but maybe they would write instead. Sometimes it seemed she'd spent her whole life waiting for things that never came. But this one, like little Tammy, would. If they told her to come in today, she'd collect the cheque this morning, get back to town and open a bank account. They would give her a chequebook and she'd go and pay for the holiday.

There was a cough from Mum's bedroom. A man's cough. Eddie had stayed over. Just like old times, except that Curt wasn't here to jump on their bed in the morning. He'd spent the night in hospital. There were no broken bones, so he'd probably be discharged later today. Then the police would be round to question him again. Julie would have to help her brother think of a good story.

The post was late. Listlessly, Julie watched television with Tammy. An actress who used to be on *Brookside* explained why she'd had silicone implants in her breasts. A pop star who Julie used to like when she was six talked about his latest comeback, but there were crow's feet around his eyes and deadness behind them. They played a bit of his song but Julie turned the telly off because she thought she heard someone in the street. Then came the creak of the letterbox opening and the soft plop of a letter landing on the carpet. It was nearly nine. Julie picked it up, a single brown envelope with red type in the window. Notice of disconnection. They couldn't afford to pay the phone bill.

Julie found herself bursting into tears. The next thing she knew, Eddie was beside her, fully dressed. She buried her head in his chest.

"It's all getting to you, Jules, but we'll sort it out. Uncle Eddie'll help." He wiped her face for her. "Your black eye's going down. You'll look right as rain by the time you go to Spain. All the fellas'll be after you."

Julie attempted a smile, failed. "Do you really want to come with us?" she asked him.

"If your mum'll have me. I could do with a break. Would you like me along?"

"Yes," Julie said. "Yes, I would."

She'd also like it if Mum got back together with Eddie, though it was less likely than Forest winning the league this season.

"My dad came round the other day," Julie told him.

"My fault, I'm afraid. He rang me and I told him about the win. You see, your mum called when she'd had a few, and – you know how it is – the story grew and grew. I heard you sent Dan packing, though."

"Yeah," Julie said, with a smile, then asked, "Where are you living now?"

"Here and there. But your mum's got my mobile number, if you ever want to talk to me. Any time, sweetheart – you know you can rely on me."

Julie nodded. Eddie changed his tone. "About the newsagent. I want you to give him a call. Tell him you're collecting the cheque this morning."

Julie was confused.

"But I'm not. I don't understand. Why should I tell him I am?"

"Trust me, darlin'."

Clare told DI Greasby what she'd found out about Eddie Broom.

"Should I call Solihull?"

"Sure. But don't be surprised if they bite your head off for wasting their valuable time. Then I've got some stuff I want you to load into the computer."

Clare was about to say that she wasn't a filing

clerk, but bit her lip. She wanted to make herself indispensable and would do whatever she had to.

It took her ages to get anyone from the task force on the line. She eventually spoke to a DC who sounded no more experienced than her. Even he tried to get her to call back later. Clare flirted with him, making it sound like he'd be doing her a big favour if he passed on her nugget of a clue.

"All right, I'll put the info on the Sergeant's desk. But I have to tell you, if this bloke's one of the gang, the last thing he'd do is let himself get caught speeding, three times, in the area of the burglaries."

"Maybe, but —"

"To be honest with you, the likelihood is that we'll be dropping Nottingham from the investigation. Doesn't quite fit the pattern."

"You mean because they used a knife, not a gun?"

"That's part of it. Thing is, we haven't given it to the press yet, but there was another one last night. Fits their MO perfectly. But it's less than a week after the Nottingham job and the gang always takes at least a month between burglaries. So it looks like yours was a copycat."

Clare tried to get more details out of the DC about the new burglary, but the guy wouldn't play. After he'd hung up on her, she told Greasby what had been said.

"Great," he said, sarcastically. "Looks like we'll have to—"

He was interrupted by the phone. Clare was about to go, but he motioned her to wait.

"All right, thanks." He put the phone down and spoke to Clare. "Get over to Central police station. They've picked up a shoplifter that I want you to interview."

"Since when did CID deal with shoplifters?" Clare asked. "Central isn't even part of our area."

"They rang me as a favour," Greasby told her. "And I haven't told you who the shoplifter is yet. It's Natalie Loscoe."

"I'm collecting the cheque this morning," Julie said, down the phone. "I'm opening a bank account when I come back. I'll have the money for you."

"No you won't," Satnam said.

"What do you mean?"

"They take three working days to clear a cheque. Earliest you'll get your money is Tuesday."

Eddie whispered in her ear. Julie repeated what he told her.

"I've made special arrangements with the bank because we're going away. Lottery cheques don't bounce, so it won't be a problem. Can you meet me—"

"No. You come to the shop," Satnam said.

Again, Eddie whispered in her ear.

"No," Julie repeated. "I don't feel safe, not after what you did to Curt."

"You don't think I was stupid enough to do that myself, do you? OK, after the shop's shut. Seven. But somewhere neutral. I'm not coming to your house."

"The embankment," Julie said, at Eddie's urging. "I'll meet you by the snack bar. Seven-thirty."

Natalie Loscoe was unrepentant.

"I was hoping it'd be the good-looking bloke," she told Clare when she picked her up.

"Who do you mean? DC Foster?"

"That's him. Is my dad coming to get me?"

"No. I'll drive you home. Why did you take those things, Natalie? Mum and Dad not give you enough pocket money?"

Natalie shrugged. "Something to do."

She'd skived off school at lunchtime, walked down Mansfield Road and spent the afternoon hanging out in the Victoria Shopping Centre, which was a magnet for skivers and kids suspended from school. Natalie slipped two lipsticks from Boots into her jacket pocket. The security cameras missed her. Then, when she walked out of River Island with a leather skirt stuffed in her schoolbag, an alarm had gone off. She'd taken off one security tag, but missed the other.

"What was the skirt for, Natalie?" Clare asked, when she'd got her in the car. "Boyfriend to impress?"

"Maybe."

"Mum and Dad wouldn't let you dress like that, I guess."

"You guess right. What's going to happen to me? Will I be charged?"

"I don't know," Clare said. "Have you ever been caught before?"

"Not really."

Meaning she had, but the police weren't involved. This time, she would be called back into the station and cautioned. But Clare didn't tell Natalie this. Let the girl sweat it out. There were other things that Clare wanted to discuss.

"There's a chance we'll go lighter on you because of what happened at the weekend," Clare said, in a softer voice. "You were tied up, weren't you?"

"For more than an hour."

"That must have been dreadful."

"I thought one of them might come back and cut me."

"You actually saw the knife, did you?"

"That's right."

"Are you sure that they didn't have any other weapons with them?"

"What like? A gun?"

Clare kept her eyes on the road ahead.

"I dunno. Maybe."

"There might have been a gun. It happened so quickly. Would it look better if I'd been threatened with a gun?"

"A knife seems scary enough to me," Clare said. "Are you having bad dreams?"

"I always have bad dreams," Natalie replied, as they turned into the driveway of the house. Clare had to get out and ask for the gates to be opened.

Maxine Loscoe shouted at Natalie for a couple of minutes then sent her up to her room.

"Aren't you the officer who found me?" she said to Clare, when her daughter was gone.

"Yes. With my partner."

"I never got the chance to thank you."

"Just doing my job. How's your head?"

"Much better, thanks."

"I don't suppose you've remembered anything else about Saturday night?"

Maxine looked flustered. "I don't seem to have done much but remember Saturday night. I've spoken to you lot three or four times, and those detectives from Birmingham twice. Why? Was there something in particular you wanted to know?"

Clare hesitated. She really ought to run this by the boss, but he had sent her to see Natalie, and they couldn't keep going back to Maxine.

"In the van, you were hit on the back of the head. Did you see what with?"

"No. I was blindfolded. It was something hard, heavy – made of metal."

"When they were talking, did they refer to weapons at all?"

"How do you mean?"

"Any reference to shooters, hardware…"

"You mean, guns? I don't remember. I was so scared, I didn't take in much of the conversation. But they definitely held a knife to my throat in the van."

Of course you'd use a knife in that situation, Clare thought. You wouldn't want people to hear a gun going off. The Asda car park was surrounded by houses. Why couldn't the Task Force see that this was the same team?

"Why are you going on about this?" Maxine asked. "Do they usually use guns? Is that it?"

Clare didn't reply. She got a list from her pocket.

"These are the people your husband said might have a grudge against the family for winning the Lottery. Could you have a look to see if there's anyone he's missed off?"

Maxine went down the names.

"No, I can't think of anyone. And some of the people on here, there's no way that they… Gordon does exaggerate sometimes."

Clare smiled reassuringly.

"I think the name Eddie Broom was mentioned. Should he be on that list?"

"Eddie? No. He and Gordon are still—"

Before Maxine could finish, Natalie came bounding downstairs, looking flushed. Her mother was angry. "I told you to stay in your room."

Natalie spoke in an excited, out-of-breath, flurry of words.

"They've done another one. And you'll never guess who. Candia Arnold!"

Candia Arnold was a twenty-year-old supermodel, with the body of a tall twelve-year-old and the face of a 1950s starlet. She'd been a star since she was seventeen. Neil used to fancy her, before he started going out with Clare and decided that he preferred the fuller figure. Candia was from Birmingham. The media sometimes mocked her accent – Cockney was more acceptable, for some reason – which made her even more popular in the Midlands, where she kept a house. The five bedroomed "cottage" was a stone's throw from a golf course (for her equally famous boyfriend), ten minutes' drive from her parents (for her) and five minutes from Birmingham International airport (for both of them). It was also within four minutes' drive of three major motorways.

Solihull was giving out no information about the burglary. Everything that Nottingham CID knew came from the radio and TV news. It seemed that Candia and her boyfriend, a black soul star from Coventry, had gone back to their "cottage" to chill out for a few days. They went to a nearby pub for a drink with friends, but returned to the house just after closing time. Armed men were waiting in the shadows. They charged in as soon as Candia had turned off the house's security system. The boy-friend was tied up. Then two of the men took Candia to a cashpoint machine while the remaining one ransacked the house.

The one remarkable thing, as far as Neil was concerned, was that, rather than hitting Candia over the head, then dumping her, the team had returned the supermodel to the house and tied her up, too. The couple had been released after an anonymous tip-off ten hours later. So, once again, the gang had broken their pattern.

"Do Solihull reckon that this job's the real McCoy?" Neil asked Greasby.

"So they told Clare. They also said it was so soon after the Loscoe job that ours must have been a copy."

"Maybe," Neil said. "Or maybe they've had someone watching the house for a while, then Candia suddenly returns to the country, so they decide to grab the opportunity, despite having done another one five days before."

"Maybe," Greasby told him. "Let's see if that occurs to Solihull. Meanwhile, you're still on the Loscoe case. Check out the guy Clare was on about."

"Eddie Broom. Clare had him linked to three of the earlier cases. So, if he's our man, then it would prove the Nottingham job was genuine."

"I know," the DI said, with a smile. "Be sweet, wouldn't it?"

10

Satnam arrived at seven, bang on time. He wasn't alone. The gorilla with him was white, with a beer belly even bigger than his chest. When Satnam saw that Julie didn't have anyone with her, he motioned to the man to stand back.

The snack bar was closed and the road was quiet. There were empty playing fields around them, with a game of five-a-side audible in the distance. Beyond the fields was the Meadows area, which included the Maynard Estate on one side, and the River Trent on the other. A Mercedes was parked 100 yards down the road. A man with a dog stood beside it, as though about to go for a walk.

"Does he know what this is about?" Julie hissed, pointing at the heavy.

"No. But he will if you try anything funny. You or Curt's mates."

"Curt's still in hospital. They kept him in another day because they're worried about internal injuries."

"Aah," Satnam said sarcastically. "My arm's much better, thanks."

"You haven't told anyone?"

Down the road, the man with the dog was getting into his car. Satnam shook his head.

"The Lottery office phoned today, to confirm that I'd sold you the ticket. That's standard practice with big wins, in case there have been tickets stolen, or some kind of fraud."

"Uh huh," Julie said.

"I told them they'd left it a bit late, as you were collecting your cheque this morning."

"Mmm." Julie was becoming nervous.

"That's right, isn't it? You got the cheque this morning?"

The grey Mercedes was driving towards them.

"I –"

"Was there a problem drawing the money from the bank?"

As the Mercedes came closer, Julie reached into her handbag, the signal that everything was OK.

"No problem," she muttered.

"All right," Satnam said. "Let's have it."

The Mercedes accelerated and swerved, knocking

Satnam's hired heavy to the ground. Then there was a squeal of brakes and the car spun round, stopping less than a metre from the newsagent. Eddie Broom got out. Satnam swore.

"What the –"

Eddie took out a gun and pointed it at Satnam.

"Do as I say and you won't be hurt. Get in the passenger seat and do up the seat belt. Julie, watch him."

Trembling, Satnam did as he was told. Eddie got out of the car and went up to the heavy, who was trying to stand up. He looked dazed.

"I wouldn't move if I were you," Eddie said. "I think you've broken a couple of ribs. Your boss'll be back for you later."

Then he held the gun by its barrel and, using it as a cosh, clobbered the man on the back of the head. He collapsed instantly. Eddie got into the driver's seat of the Merc. Julie sat in the back.

"All right, Satnam," Eddie said. "We're going for a little ride."

That evening, Ruth and Clare went to see Steve's play, which neither of them enjoyed much, although Steve turned out to be a reasonably good actor. He invited them for a drink afterwards, but neither girl went along. Sam would be meeting him in the pub. They didn't want to be there when she gave him the push. The phone was ringing when they got in. Ruth answered, hoping it would be Ben, whose shift was nearly over. But it was Ben's boss, wanting Clare.

"You interviewed that newsagent earlier in the week, didn't you?"

"Yes," Clare said. "He wasn't at all co-operative, though. Why?"

"I've had his wife on the phone. Seems he's disappeared. You interested?"

"Yes," Clare said. "I am."

"I'll drive by and pick you up before I go over there."

Mrs Singh looked ten years younger than her husband, younger, even, than Clare. She had two small children, both of whom were in bed, but could be heard crying.

"You say he went out to meet someone?" Clare asked, in her gentlest voice. "But you don't know who?"

"No. He said it was business and he wouldn't be long. I was bathing the children. I didn't pay close attention."

"How long ago was this?" Clare asked.

"He went out just before seven, nearly three hours ago."

"I have to ask because I came to see your husband earlier in the week. Do you think that his visit could be connected with the beating he got on Monday?"

Mrs Singh frowned.

"Some boys tried to mug my husband early one morning and, when he wouldn't give them the float from the till, they kicked him a few times."

"Did you see this happen?"

"No, but he told me about it immediately afterwards."

"It's not what he told us," Clare commented.

"What did he tell you?" Mrs Singh demanded.

"Nothing."

"My husband is not fond of the police. He had some little troubles when he was a teenager. Perhaps –"

They went through a string of questions, trying to establish where Satnam Singh might have gone. The best bet, in a case like this, was that he was with a girlfriend and had got carried away. He would return in the early hours with a lame excuse, and police time would have been wasted. But Mrs Singh insisted that her husband rarely had time un-accounted for. She knew where he was, it seemed, every minute of the day. Except tonight.

"Anything on his mind lately?" Paul Grace asked. "Any problems?"

"Not that I know of."

"Anything – doesn't matter how small."

Mrs Singh thought.

"He had a couple of phone calls from the National Lottery with a query about a ticket he sold. I asked him what they wanted but he wouldn't talk about it, said it wasn't important. But the money from the Lottery is a big part of our income. If they took away our franchise –"

There was a message for Paul on the radio. Clare heard Gary's voice.

"We were just doing a last circuit before knocking off when we found this bloke, by the side of the road. Ambulance is on the way, but it looks like he's concussed, probably broken a couple of ribs. The guy can't or won't say what hit him, but he's been there for a couple of hours."

"Why are you calling me?" Grace asked. "It sounds like a hit and run, or a drunken fight."

"We asked what he was doing there in the first place. The guy told us that he was minding an Asian newsagent."

"We're on our way," Paul told him, then spoke to Mrs Singh. "If we find out anything, anything at all, I'll call you. If your husband shows up, or calls, or you remember anything that you haven't already told us, call me straight away."

"Of course."

They got to the embankment just as the minder was being put into an ambulance.

"Rejoined us, have you?" Gary asked Clare.

"Just for the evening."

"Get anything else out of him?" Paul asked John Farraday.

"The newsagent paid him twenty quid. He was

told the job would take half an hour, an hour at the most. He's meant to be on the door at a pub down the road. What's interesting is who he says the newsagent was meeting."

"Who?"

"A girl. Very pretty girl, the guy said, seventeen or eighteen. Wearing sunglasses."

The day had been dull, overcast.

"As a disguise?" Clare ventured.

Gary shrugged. "You tell me."

Paul looked around. "Witnesses?"

"No one's come forward. I was thinking of asking in the pub, but –" He looked at his watch. The shift ended in two minutes.

"You go back to the station, brief the night shift. Clare and I'll have a look round."

Paul turned to Clare when they'd gone.

"I've been missing you all week. At least now we'll get to have a drink together."

No one in the pub had seen anything. Paul and Clare sat in a corner looking out on to the river. It was odd, Clare found, being with Paul in uniform, when she wasn't. He looked a lot older than her.

"What can you do at twenty-one that you can't do before?" she asked him.

"Be an MP. That's about it."

"Doesn't appeal."

"And drink in a bar in the USA."

"That sounds more like it." Clare smiled.

"Have you ever been there?"

"The furthest I've ever been is Naples. You?"

Paul nodded. "When I was a student. I spent a summer over there. Best summer of my life. I'd love to go back. We could go, next year."

"You seem pretty sure that we'll still be together next year."

He looked sad for a moment.

"I wasn't –" Clare blundered. "I didn't mean... I mean, I'd love to go to the States, with you. But we've only been together for –"

"Four weeks on Saturday," Paul said. "I'm sorry. You're right. It's not long. But I like to push things. I can't help it. And I'm crazy about you."

Clare felt embarrassed.

"Let's talk about the newsagent," she said.

"Yes. I thought we'd call in on Mrs Singh on our way back, just in case he's shown up."

"Fine. Have you any idea what it's about?"

"Not a clue. But you're the detective now."

Clare rested her chin on her left fist and thought aloud.

"I was wondering about the Lottery," she said. "Mrs Singh mentioned it, and someone on the estate won £50,000 the other day, Gary told me. There was some trouble with her brother being beaten up."

"The Wilder girl," Paul said. "Ben mentioned that he'd seen her with a black eye. You think that

116

could be connected with the newsagent?"

"It doesn't make sense," Clare told him. "Three beatings, four if you count the bouncer tonight, all because someone won the Lottery."

"Gambling arouses passions," Paul told her. "Do you play it?"

"No. On principle. I think it's bad for people."

"It's certainly bad value," Paul said, giving her the gambler's perspective. "Only forty-five per cent of your stake comes back in prizes. The real winners are the government. They take tax on every ticket. Not only that, but money goes on 'good causes' that should have been government-funded in the first place, if they're so important. It's not a gamble, it's a rip-off."

"Try telling Julie Wilder that."

"Point taken," Paul replied. "Scratch cards are better value. The return's fifty-five per cent. But those are still rubbish odds compared to roulette. Most people are throwing money at an impossible dream."

"Not impossible for Gordon Loscoe," Clare pointed out. "What other chance have the Wilders or Loscoes got of getting rich? It's better than nothing."

"I suppose so," Paul said, being conciliatory, "when you put it that way. But I'll never play it. Do you know that guy? He's staring at you."

Clare turned round and shuddered. It was Max, her first boyfriend, looking as smooth and self-satisfied as ever. He was with a girl who looked barely old enough to drink, but it was Clare he was gaping at. He waved. Clare faked half a smile in return.

"I used to know him," she told Paul. "But I don't want to any more." Too late. Max was coming over. He was as good-looking as ever, and knew it.

"Clare! You're looking great! It's been too long."

Clare introduced Paul, who smiled unconvincingly. A message was coming in on his radio.

"Excuse me," he said. "I'll take this outside, where it's quiet."

"I saw you in town a while back," Max said, "with a bloke who looked like a copper. And now… What is it, have you got a thing about the uniform?"

Clare wasn't having this. She pulled her warrant card from her hip pocket. Max faked amazement.

"Oh, I see! You're one of them. That explains it. I'd love to see you in uniform. I'll bet it's a real turn-on. Want to go out for a drink soon? We had some good times, didn't we? Here comes your boss."

"He's not my boss," Clare said. "He's my boyfriend. But he *is* on duty, and I'm going to get him to go over and ask your girlfriend for her birth certificate. That is, unless you leave me alone, now."

Max backed away as Paul sat down.

"Trouble?"

"No."

Paul drained his drink. "Time we were moving. Satnam's shown up, at home."

In the car, Paul asked her about Max. "You two were an item once, weren't you? I could tell."

"Briefly. A long time ago."

"But he's still interested."

"I'm not."

"Blokes like him always get up my nose," Paul confided. "Tall, full of it. They get all the best-looking girls without even trying. Girls like you. I saw him walk up to you and thought, *I've had it now*."

"Don't be daft."

She squeezed his thigh.

"I'm not tall," Paul protested. "I'm not handsome. All my life I've worked hard to become something, to give me an edge. And I've succeeded. But, out of uniform, I'm just another bloke."

"Nonsense," Clare said. "And, if you're running yourself down in order to fish for a compliment, forget it."

She saw from the sadness that flickered across his face that she'd got it wrong. His low self-esteem was genuine. But it was too late to say anything about that now. They were parking behind the news-agent's shop.

"He doesn't want to talk to you," Mrs Singh told Paul. "It was a misunderstanding – a family meeting I'd forgotten about."

"I see," Paul said.

"I'm sorry for wasting your time."

"That's perfectly all right, but we would like to see your husband, to make sure that he's all right."

"He's fine. But he had to go out again."

Paul frowned.

"There's also the matter of the man who was run over. He'll need to make a statement about that."

"I see."

"Could you have him come into the station at ten tomorrow?" Clare asked. "Your rush should have died down by then."

"Who should he ask for?"

"Detective Constable Coppola."

"What do you think's going on?" Clare asked Paul, as he drove her home.

"You tell me. You're the detective."

Clare ignored the jibe and told Paul her latest idea.

"The girl in sunglasses. Suppose it was Julie Wilder, with her black eye?"

"What would she want with Satnam? He sold her the ticket. She'd be grateful."

"Suppose there was something dodgy about the ticket?" Clare suggested. "Say it was actually forged, or stolen. Say Satnam didn't really sell it?"

"You've got a point," Paul conceded. "Stolen scratch cards are practically impossible to identify. If someone somehow nicked a bunch of cards – Curt, for instance – and took the winning ones to a different outlet, they'd pay up. The only difficulty comes if one of the cards were to win a big prize. Then, the Lottery organizers would do a careful check to authenticate it. They'd look into stolen cards."

"There's a problem, though," Clare pointed out.

"What?"

"Satnam hasn't reported any cards stolen."

"True. Maybe you'll come up with a better theory when you question him tomorrow."

He had stopped outside the house. Clare undid her seat belt and he undid his. Then they kissed, passionately.

"Are you going to invite me in?" Paul asked as they slipped apart. It was just after 11pm. Clare thought for a moment. She'd welcome the chance to talk about the case some more. But she could tell that Paul had other ideas. And so might she. Clare had to be up early in the morning. She used a line from a half-remembered old movie.

"I always think it's wise to leave something for another time, don't you?"

"I'll keep you to that," Paul said, kissing her again.

"Another time," she repeated, reluctantly getting out of his car.

11

Julie was scared. She hadn't realized that Uncle Eddie carried a gun, or that he'd use his car as a weapon. Satnam had been scared, too. But would he stay scared when Eddie wasn't around? And the newsagent had been right about one thing. She'd asked at the bank. The cheque, when she got it, would take at least three working days to clear. So, if she collected it today, Friday, she wouldn't be able to draw on the money until Wednesday. The holiday, therefore, had to be delayed for a week. That meant another week of hanging around on the Maynard Estate.

Another week when anything could happen.

Eddie came downstairs at eight in the morning.

"You'd better ring the Lottery office as soon as it opens," he told Julie. "If there're any problems, I want to know, so I can sort the Paki."

"I suppose," Julie said, with distaste. She didn't like the newsagent, but there was no need to bring his race into the discussion. She didn't like difficult phone calls either, but, just after nine, she called the Lottery office. It took three conversations before she got through to the right person.

"Miss Wilder, yes. Your payment should be authorized today. We'll ring you as soon as —"

"But I was told —"

"I'm sorry. There have been delays due to staff being on holiday. If you could bear with us..."

Julie was still trying to work out what to say next when she realized that the woman had hung up.

Ruth stayed up after her night shift while Gary and Sam got up early so that they could all have breakfast with Clare on her birthday. Sam had bought her a beautiful dress, Ruth a pair of Ray-Ban sunglasses. She put them on together and felt like a film star, albeit one who had to be in the office at nine.

"These are wonderful. You shouldn't have spent so much money. I'll wear the dress tomorrow. Oh, this is fantastic!"

Gary gave her a huge bunch of lilies. Sam cooked her scrambled eggs with grilled tomatoes and bacon on toast. Neil was taking her to lunch and Mum and Dad were cooking for her tonight, so Clare worried whether she'd fit into the dress by tomorrow. But she'd rarely started a day in a better mood.

"We had a whip round," Chris Dylan said when she got in to work.

"I didn't expect —"

Most officers didn't write cards, never mind give presents, when it was someone's birthday. It just wasn't part of the culture.

"Ah, but we've never had a twenty-first before. We wanted to mark the occasion. So you'll find a little something inside this card."

The other officers broke into an impromptu chorus of "Happy birthday to you". Clare opened the card, which contained a cheerfully obscene cartoon, whose punchline she could guess without reading it. When she looked to see who'd signed it, several slips of paper fell out.

"What are these?" Clare asked the Sergeant.

"Lottery tickets. We heard how much you like the Lottery, so we got you eight lucky dips."

Clare gave them her best ironic smile and said "Thank you" politely.

Satnam Singh didn't show up for his interview. Clare rang the newsagent's, where his wife said he was on his way. When Neil came back from the Maynard Estate, Clare asked if he'd seen him.

"Nope. I've been looking for Eddie Broom, but he's not been at the address on his driving licence for two years." He dumped a couple of photos on

Clare's desk. "No one seems to think he lives there any more, but it might be worth asking around after lunch. Maybe we can track down your newsagent at the same time."

"Don't bother," Clare said.

Satnam was walking over to her desk. He looked, she was surprised to find, in perfect health.

"You wanted to see me?"

"Yes. About last night. I'll find an interview room."

"No need," Satnam said. "There's nothing to tell. Nothing happened."

"That's not the way I hear it," Clare said. "And it doesn't explain why you hired a bouncer to protect you – or fail to protect you – when you went to the embankment last night."

"Look," Satnam said. "I had a threatening phone call. I thought it might be connected to a bunch of boys who tried to mug me on Monday. The phone call told me to be at the embankment at a certain time, or my shop would be burnt down. I thought it was a joke, kids mucking about. But I took some protection with me, just to be on the safe side."

"You didn't think to call the police?" Clare asked.

"No. I said I thought it was somebody playing silly beggars and I was right. No one came. I spoke to a girl who was passing and she hadn't seen anybody waiting. So I left. Shortly afterwards, the bouncer I'd hired was careless and got knocked over by a car. But that was coincidence, an accident."

Clare didn't believe a word of it. She wanted to know why the newsagent was lying.

"Tell me about the phone call."

"It sounded like a boy. Like I said, I didn't take it seriously."

She pressed him, but got no further. Then she asked if he'd ever had any scratch cards stolen.

"No. They're kept well behind the counter. The only people with access to them are myself, my wife and my niece, who helps out. There's no risk."

"Yet the National Lottery office has been ringing you this week. What was that about?"

For a moment, Satnam looked flustered.

"They were checking that I sold a card that won a big prize. It's standard practice."

"And the scratch card was bought by –?"

"Julie Wilder."

"OK," Clare said. "Thanks, for now. I might have more questions after I've been to the hospital."

The confident look on Satnam's face told Clare that he'd already squared his story with the minder. As he was getting up to go, Neil came over.

"Could you take a look at these," he asked Satnam, "and tell me if you've seen this guy around recently?"

Satnam picked up the two photographs of Eddie Broom. One was five years old, the other nearly ten. Satnam's face dropped and he blinked several times.

"I know him," he said, finally. "You know that. I mentioned his name to you the other day: Eddie. But I haven't seen him for years."

He left hurriedly.

When Curt came out of hospital, he seemed changed. Physically, the beating hadn't done him serious harm – the doctors had made sure of that. But mentally, Julie could tell, he had been given a serious scare.

"I'm sorry I didn't visit," she told him, when they were alone in the living room together. "But Tammy –"

"I know," Curt said. "Mum told me you didn't get the money yet."

Mum was at work.

"It won't be till Monday, now."

"Where's Uncle Eddie?"

"I don't know."

She hadn't seen Uncle Eddie since he told her to get out of the car the night before. Then he'd driven off with his gun, a borrowed Alsatian and the kidnapped newsagent. Julie told Curt about it.

"He said, if anyone asked, I was at home. Mum'll back that up."

"Your eye's looking better," Curt said, almost tenderly.

"Thanks. I told school you wouldn't be in before Monday."

Curt grinned. "A week on Monday, you mean. Do you think Eddie's killed him?"

"Satnam? No. At least I hope not."

"Me neither," Curt said, to her surprise.

"No?"

"No. With all that sitting around in bed, I worked a few things out. I shouldn't have done him over. If you and me had gone to him in the first place, and offered him a few quid, none of this would have happened."

"It's too late now," Julie told him.

"I guess you're right," Curt admitted. "What do you think Eddie's done?"

"Scared the life out of him, I suppose. Threatened to kill his wife, or kids, or both. I'd never realized how frightening Eddie could be until I saw him with that gun in his hands."

Curt kind of laughed, but he wasn't really amused.

"What do you think he's into now, Eddie? With the gun and all that?"

"There's only one thing it can be," Julie told him.

"You mean –?"

He made a gesture by crooking his little finger.

"Yeah. I mean armed robbery."

Neil was glad to get Clare to himself at lunch. They talked over the morning's work.

"The story about the car accident was complete cobblers," Clare commented.

"As was his not having seen Eddie Broom for years. Did you see his face?"

"The question is," Clare said, "who's trying to deprive Julie Wilder of her fifty thousand pounds?"

"Why don't we ring the Lottery office when we get back?" Neil suggested. "See if she's actually got the money yet."

"Good idea."

"But, before that," Neil got out a small, delicately wrapped package, "happy twenty-first," he said, and raised his glass to her.

Clare unwrapped the fancy paper, then opened the tiny box inside.

"Oh, Neil. This is perfect." It was a brooch. A large, pale opal mounted on an antique silver setting. "But you shouldn't have."

"I wanted to."

Actually, he had bought it months before, after finding the brooch downstairs in Top Hat Antiques, on the Derby Road. Back then, he had been trying to work up the nerve to ask Clare to marry him. Eventually, he'd asked, and been turned down. He'd thought of giving the brooch to Melanie, his new girlfriend, but it didn't seem right somehow. Now Clare was putting it on.

"It looks great on you."

"Thanks." She leant over and kissed him affectionately, on the lips. It was the first such kiss he'd had from her since they split up, and it moved him.

"We'd better be getting back," he said.

"Yes. Do you mind if I —?"

"No. Take it off." He didn't want the guys in the CID office to see the brooch and guess who it came from, either.

"There's something I've been meaning to tell you," Clare said, as she got into his car. "Before you hear it from someone else."

"You're seeing someone?"

"Yes."

"I hope it works out."

"Thanks."

They drove back to the station in silence. Neil didn't want to know anything about the guy she was dating. He didn't know how seeing Clare with someone new would affect him. Probably the guy would be at the party tomorrow, which was why Clare had warned him. That was considerate of her. Neil would go. He owed her that much. But he wouldn't stay for long.

Ben was beginning his last shift before going on holiday. Ruth was taking her holiday from today. Tonight, they would meet at his flat, celebrate their freedom. Ben had a couple of videos rented, a litre of Asda's best Italian red, and a family-size Four Seasons pizza.

Ben walked past the newsagent's where, through the window, Satnam Singh was selling a teenager ten cigarettes. Ben had a quick look to check the girl's age. You got the odd complaint. There'd been something going on last night, with Satnam supposedly missing, but it seemed to have been a false alarm. The boss, Paul Grace, had hinted as much at briefing, adding that the matter was now in the hands of CID. Maybe, when Ben saw Neil and Clare tomorrow, he would find out what it was all about.

Thinking of Neil, Ben felt guilty. The two men hadn't gone out for a drink together for a month. They were what you might call best friends. However, Ben had neglected to tell Neil that Clare was seeing his former boss, Paul Grace. True, Neil and Clare split up a while ago, and Neil was seeing Melanie, but Ben knew how he would feel if he found out that his ex was seeing someone new.

"Hey, Ben!" Neil and Clare materialized in front of him, getting out of a CID car.

"What brings you to these parts?" he asked them.

"There's somebody we're trying to track down," Neil said. "He might even be involved in last night's shenanigans: Eddie Broom. He's from round here."

"Before my time," Ben told them.

Clare held out a photograph. "Recognize him?"

Ben knew the face straight away.

"I do. I saw him last night, on my rounds. Drives a big grey Merc. I watched him get out of it."

"Where?"

"He was going into the Wilders'."

131

12

Neil parked two streets away from the Wilder house, then Clare walked over and cautiously peered around the corner: no grey Mercedes. Neil rang DI Greasby while Clare and Ben talked.

"Have you got any idea what's going on here?" Ben asked.

"Not really. But Eddie Broom is a mate of Gordon Loscoe's. We're hoping that, somehow, he's tied up with the robbery there."

"And the motorway team?"

"Maybe. But the Task Force thinks we're wasting our time."

Neil returned. "Boss doesn't want us to go in. He wants us to keep watch, discreetly. He said he'll authorize the overtime."

"But it's my birthday!" Clare complained. "I'm

having dinner with Mum and Dad. Then –"

"You do the first watch," Neil offered. "Then I'll take over. Ben, do you know anyone round here who's reasonably friendly to us?"

Ben thought for a minute.

"There's this bloke lives a couple of doors away from the Wilders, Nigel, who reported some trouble the other night. He might co-operate."

"Think you could go and ask?"

"I can try."

Clare felt conspicuous, standing on the end of the next street, waiting for Ben to get a result. True, she and Neil were in plain clothes, but they had both worked the beat in this area. Anyone might recognize them. Ben radioed them from round the corner.

"All right, you can go in the back door. There's an alley. The number eleven's painted on the gate. I'm going to work my way down the street. There's a stolen van been dumped at the other end. I'll ask a few questions. It'll explain why I knocked on Nigel's door and give me a chance to look in the Wilder house."

Neil and Clare sat in Nigel's bedroom, staring through its net curtains. "How long you gonna need to stay?" the house's owner asked.

"Until this guy shows up," Neil told him. "After five, we'll work shifts. If he's not turned up by midnight, we'll call it quits. Is that OK by you?"

"I won't be in bed before four anyhow."

Five o'clock approached. Neil listened as Clare rang her mum and explained why she'd be late.

"How are they?" he asked, when she'd finished.

He'd grown fond of Clare's parents over the past two years, and they of him. In a way, they'd treated him like a son. Neither had really recovered from Angelo's death.

"Mum's much the same. Dad's not so happy. Business didn't pick up as well as he'd hoped over the summer. Now autumn's in sight and, reading between the lines, he's got quite a few debts. They've given up on trying to sell the house, can't afford to move somewhere more expensive."

She stopped, a cloud crossing her face, which made Neil wish he hadn't asked this question on her birthday.

"How's your mum?" she asked.

"Fine."

"Does she get on with –"

"Melanie? They haven't met yet. I visited her parents, though. Boy, they were hard work."

Clare smiled, accepting the sideways compliment to her own family.

"Look," Neil offered. "If you really want to get away –"

"No. It's fine. I'll stay here till eight. Come in tomorrow, if necessary. You go now. Make that call to the Lottery office before they close. I'll be fine."

Neil waited until he saw Ben knocking on the door of the Wilder house.

"Happy birthday," he repeated, before going downstairs and sneaking out through the back alley.

"Oh," Julie said. "It's you."

"Hello again. I'm just making a few enquiries."

"You'd better come in."

The tall, black copper was even more handsome in uniform than out, she decided.

"Your eye seems to be a lot better," the PC commented.

"Yeah. It looked worse than it was."

"I'm not so sure about that."

For a few moments, she had a sudden urge to tell him everything: the truth about the Lottery ticket, who had hit her, Uncle Eddie, the lot. But he was a policeman.

"Anyone else at home?"

"Just the baby. She's asleep upstairs. Why? Who did you want to see?"

"Anybody who's living here."

"What's it about?"

He told her about a van that was parked at the end of the street. Julie hadn't even noticed it, she admitted.

"Maybe I could ask your mother, or Curt."

"Curt's been in hospital. I s'pose it's possible Mum saw something, but she doesn't like talking to the police."

The handsome black man smiled.

"That's not unusual round here. Anyone else been staying, might have seen something?"

Julie hesitated. Uncle Eddie had been here for two nights, and would be coming back tonight, too. But she wasn't sure whether to tell the officer. Suppose he was digging for something other than the van?

"Anything wrong?"

"No. It's only ... my boyfriend used to stay, but we split up this week. That's how I got the black eye."

"He didn't want to split up with you?"

"He didn't want to split up with my money."

The officer smiled sympathetically.

"Got that holiday sorted yet?"

"I'm waiting to collect the cheque. We'll be off a week on Sunday, with a bit of luck."

"I hope you have a good time. And, if you remember anything –" He gave her the number of his station and his name: Ben Shipman.

"I'll do that," she said, and showed Ben to the door. "When are you off?"

"Sunday."

"Enjoy yourself."

"Thanks."

He glanced back at her as she was shutting the door. Julie gave him a shy smile. He fancied her, she could tell, and was flattered by it. But he would never make a move. Guys like that were faithful to their girlfriends. That was part of what made him so attractive. The girlfriend would be black, like him, and a churchgoer, probably. Julie would never go out with anybody like Ben Shipman. But she could dream. Maybe, on holiday, she would meet someone who could take her away from the Maynard Estate, be a father to Tammy. Maybe, when the money came, she would make a new beginning. But she doubted it. One rule seemed to govern her life: something always got in the way.

The Lottery office, as it turned out, shut at four on Fridays. Neil left a message, then talked to Dylan and Greasby. The DI asked to be paged if Eddie Broom showed up at the Wilders'.

"I'd like to get a decent lead," the DI said, "put Solihull's noses out."

Neil wondered how Clare was getting on. He should have offered to do the full eight hours, but something had stopped him. His days of bending over backwards to help Clare were over.

Someone had stuck a photo of Candia Arnold on the noticeboard, half-naked in an ad for unisex perfume, or cologne, he supposed they'd call it. Pinups were frowned upon in CID these days, but the model being burgled had given some wag the excuse he needed. Scratch a policeman, Neil thought, and you found a sexist underneath. Often you didn't even need to scratch.

The phone rang with a call for Clare. Neil took it and explained that she wasn't there.

"This is DC Church, from Solihull. She's our liaison for the Loscoe burglary."

"I don't think we've got anything new for you," Neil said. "Though we're working on a lead."

"We've got something to show you," DC Church said. "A sketch. Candia Arnold got a glimpse of one of the gang when he took his mask off to use a cash machine. We want to see if any of you lot recognize it. But this is on a need-to-know basis. If word gets around that the girl can ID one of the gang, she'd be in danger."

"Understood."

"All right. Be by the fax machine. I'm sending it now."

Neil looked at the picture, which showed a man of about forty. He was slightly balding, soft fleshed with narrow eyes. It rang no bells. But then he looked at the two photos of Eddie Broom. Add five years to one, ten to another and … it was possible. There was no point in sending the Broom photos to Brum. They would laugh at him, as they had laughed at the suggestion that Broom's speeding tickets linked him to the robberies. But, if Nottingham found the bloke, and he had no alibi, Solihull might be laughing on the other side of their faces.

Clare watched from the upstairs window, wondering when something would happen. At six, Shirley Wilder came home. She slouched down the street, cigarette in her mouth, with the demeanour of someone who'd just finished work, although Clare knew that she was signing on. Half an hour later, Curt came in. Then, nothing.

Nigel brought her mugs of tea at hourly intervals. She found herself listening to him talk about the Maynard Estate.

"They say lots of bad people live round here, but no one starts out bad. Take Curt across the road. He was a nice kid until he was nine, ten. Then he started getting a little crazy. But, you know, he always says hello to me, we have a joke now and then. Trouble is, what's the world got to offer him? He's no genius, but he's smart enough to see that there's nothing for him in Nottingham. Same with a lot of people around here. So they cheat the Social, do a little thieving or dealing. Who can blame them?"

Clare didn't argue. Put an argument like that to Jan Hunt, her mentor, and Jan would jump down your throat. But Clare thought there was some truth in what Nigel was saying.

"I know what you mean," she said. "They cut money on schools and build more and more prisons. It's crazy."

She wondered what Nigel did for a living, but knew better than to ask. In one way, Jan had taught her, the unemployed were like the criminals: they all had a sob story to tell. Better not to ask unless you really needed to know.

Nigel came upstairs again at seven-thirty. There were still no comings or goings in the Wilder house. Clare needed the loo. She'd meant to hold on till Neil came but now asked Nigel to watch for her while she used his bathroom. When she was back at the window, he asked her not to look around.

"I need to get changed."

"Going somewhere special?" she asked, as his wardrobe door opened and closed.

"Work."

"Oh?" Clare was surprised. "At this time?"

"Yeah. You can turn round. I'm decent now."

She glanced round to see that he was wearing a familiar uniform.

"That's why I live here. It's real convenient for the station."

"You're a —"

"Train driver. Hey, isn't that what you were looking for?"

"God, yes!"

A grey Mercedes was pulling up outside the Wilder house.

"I've got to go," Nigel said. "Here's a back-door key. Hide it under the bin when you leave."

In an area like the Maynard Estate, that was a ridiculously meagre security measure, but Clare didn't argue. "Thanks," she said, not looking around. "We really appreciate this."

She watched as Eddie Broom got out of the Mercedes, rang the doorbell. Shirley answered it. Was that a kiss? Eddie was holding a bottle. It didn't look like they were going anywhere for a while. Clare checked her watch. Neil would already be on his way over here. There was no point in calling his pager.

She waited for him to arrive.

Eddie, after a night away from Shirley, was all smiles and affection. He'd brought good Scotch. Julie didn't like Scotch, but had a glass anyway. When she fed Tammy later, the stuff would be in her milk, and the baby might sleep more heavily. Julie needed a good night's sleep.

Eddie was annoyed that the Lottery hadn't paid up yet. He'd really wanted to get away this weekend.

"Maybe it'd be easier if I paid for the holiday," he suggested. "We can collect the money when we get back."

"Too late," Julie told him. "I've changed the provisional bookings to next week now."

Eddie poured another drink. Shirley fixed him a sandwich. Curt was slumped in front of the TV, watching a cop show. He was sulking because Eddie had told him he was too young to drink whisky. Eddie glanced at the screen.

"The police were round earlier," Julie told him, reminded by the programme. It was best that he heard it from her. She knew, from when he had lived with them before, how paranoid Eddie could be.

"Did they ask about me?"

"No. Of course not," Julie told him. "They wanted to know about this van that was dumped at the end of the street."

"The police are always coming round," Shirley assured him, as she handed over two meat-paste sandwiches. "It's nothing to do with you."

"I have to be careful," Eddie said, "about people knowing where I am."

The commercials came on, beginning with the one for the National Lottery, the one with the pointing finger, which finished with the words, *It could be you*. Julie still found it hard to believe that it really was her. She was one of the winners.

"By the way, Uncle Eddie," she said, "where *were* you last night?"

"I had business to do after finishing with your newsagent pal. You were lucky I had time to fit him in."

That was interesting, but didn't explain where he'd spent the night.

"And where do you live when you're not living here?" Julie asked.

"She's a nosy one, isn't she?" Shirley said, sarkily.

"All you need to know," Eddie told her, draining his drink and pouring another one, "is that I'm on the other end of my mobile number. As far as the rest of it goes, I don't exist."

"But you must live somewhere," Julie argued. Eddie was silent. "I was just wondering," Julie continued, hesitantly, "what exactly you do for a living these days."

Eddie gave her an undertaker's smile.

"Believe me," he said, "you really don't want to know."

There was a sharp knock on the door. Eddie jumped to his feet.

"Filth," he said, then looked at Julie. "You sure you didn't mention me?"

"Not a word," she said. "Why would they want you, anyhow?"

Eddie scowled. Shirley was looking through the window.

"Plain clothes," she said. "Young 'uns. Do you want me to stall them?" Shirley was talking like she was on a TV cop show herself.

"No," Eddie said. "The car's out front. It's in my name, so they'll have got it off the computer. Only thing to do is front it out. Open the door."

Shirley did. Two of them stood there – an attractive, Mediterranean-looking woman with dark hair, and a slight bloke with an awkward smile. Julie thought for a moment that they couldn't be police. Maybe they were from the Lottery, come to present her cheque in person.

"We're looking for Edward Broom," the bloke said. "He was seen coming in here."

Out of their field of view, Eddie knocked back his glass of Scotch, then spoke.

"You've found me. What can I do for you?"

Now the woman spoke. At first she sounded confident, but as she went on, her voice rose a little, became too fast. Maybe they wanted Eddie for something big.

"We'd be grateful if you'd accompany us to the station, sir. There are a few matters that we think you can clear up for us."

"You'll have to do better than that," Eddie said, with a laugh.

"We're talking about abducted newsagents and bouncers with broken ribs," the bloke said.

"I see."

Eddie looked relieved. He'd been worried that they were on about something more serious. Julie wondered what it was.

"Don't finish the bottle," Eddie told Shirley, handing her a card with the name and home phone number of his solicitor on it. "I'll be back."

The two police officers took him away.

13

Eddie Broom was not co-operating. He claimed to work abroad a lot. For a permanent address, he'd offered them a box-office number.

"If you can't give us a fixed address," Greasby told him, "we're going to have to keep you overnight."

"On what grounds?"

"Withholding information."

"This isn't a police state. If you want to keep me in, you'll have to arrest me, charge me."

"That can be arranged," DI Greasby offered, in his surliest voice. Neil didn't know if he could back up the threat.

"This is all about some poxy newsagent, isn't it? Get him down here then, see what he has to say."

"There's a man in hospital."

"And he claims I put him there, does he?"

Neil looked up. Clare was signalling at the door. Neil nodded at the Inspector, who spoke into the tape recorder.

"Interview suspended at twenty-two hundred hours."

As they were leaving the room, Greasby turned round.

"Oh, I forgot to ask. Where were you last Friday night?"

Eddie Broom looked at the switched-off tape recorder.

"No comment," he said, with a frozen smile.

"His solicitor just got here," Clare said, when the two men were outside. "Have we got anything to hold him on?"

"We could keep him for twenty-four hours for running over the bouncer," Greasby said, "but they'll both know it's a joke. The victim'll never testify. I'm going to ring Solihull, see how quickly Candia Arnold can attend an identity parade. Neil, get one of those instant cameras. Take a picture of Mr Broom so that I can fax them an up-to-date one."

"Shouldn't you have gone home?" Neil asked Clare when he was through with the fax. She was meant to be at a birthday meal with her parents. Clare shrugged.

"I'm meeting someone else in a few minutes. There's no point. I rang Mum and Dad. They understand. Or say they do."

The solicitor came out of the interview room.

"I've talked to my client. He has no fixed address, but will be available at the Wilder house over the weekend should you require him. I think that's a generous offer and, given that you have no grounds on which to hold him, I must ask for him to be released now. Otherwise I will be forced to—"

"Hold your horses," Greasby said, coming back from the phone. "I'd like you to have your man at the station at eleven on Monday, for an identity parade. Will he agree to do that?"

"Who is doing the identifying?" the solicitor asked.

"I'm not at liberty to tell you that, as it may put the witness at risk. Nor will I be able to tell you on Monday."

The solicitor frowned. He probably thought that they were bringing in the bouncer, not realizing that the police were really after Eddie as a candidate for the motorway-team burglaries.

"I'll have to consult my client," he said.

"Why wait until Monday?" Neil asked, when he was gone.

"Candia Arnold's doing a shoot for *Vogue* in Milan at the moment. She won't be back until Sunday morning. Anyway, it'll take us that long to get an ID parade together. You ever tried getting stand-ins to show up at the weekend?"

The solicitor came out and said that his client agreed.

"Very well. You can take him home."

The Inspector turned to Clare.

"There's someone waiting for you. Enjoy the rest of your birthday. And good luck with the Lottery tickets."

Clare gave him a wry smile, then wished Neil goodnight.

"I'll see you both at the party, I hope."

Neil meant to linger, but, in the end, couldn't help going down the corridor after Clare. It was none of his business, but he wanted to know who she was meeting. Some long-haired young man, he expected. Maybe a student like Melanie. Or a post-graduate, more likely. Education turned her on.

But there was no young man in the station foyer, only Inspector Grace, in civvies, with a package under one arm. Neil always found the Inspector overdressed when he was out of uniform. Today was no exception. Grace wore smartly pressed Chinos over brown, Italian-looking shoes. Despite having just come off shift, he sported an immaculate white linen shirt and colourful silk tie. He could be about to walk into the Ritz.

"Sorry if I kept you waiting," Neil heard Clare say to her old boss.

"I'm just glad you could get away," the Inspector said, putting his free arm around Clare's waist and kissing her tenderly on the lips. "Happy birthday."

They walked out of the station together, arm in arm. Neil watched them from the doorway where he stood, still as a statue, feeling like he'd been shot in the heart.

"Did you see Clare today?" Ruth asked Ben, as they tucked into their pizza at his flat, after work.

"Yes."

He told her about their meeting.

"I hope you remembered to wish her a happy birthday."

"Oops."

"Oh, Ben –"

He changed the subject rapidly. "Could we drive somewhere for lunch tomorrow?"

"Sure. Did you have anywhere in mind"

"Mansfield. My parents'd like to meet you."

"Really? You told them about me?"

"I told them."

There was a mixture of joy and relief on Ruth's face, though she said nothing else. It hadn't occurred to Ben that she might be hurt by not having been introduced to his parents. After all, she never even mentioned hers.

Later, in bed, he felt guilty, and not only about keeping Ruth a secret for so long. His mind wasn't on the woman sleeping next to him, but on Julie Wilder. It was stupid. He hadn't noticed her for the past six months, but then their paths had crossed three times in a week and, each time, she'd made it clear that she fancied him. It was mutual.

Ben loved Ruth. That wasn't in doubt. But it didn't stop him from wanting other women. Julie was out of the question. She was too young. She had a child. Her mother and brother were criminals. If Ben were single, he and she might have had, at best, a brief fling. Maybe that was all she wanted.

But Ben had never had a brief fling. He had only been with two women in his life: Charlene and Ruth. Hardly surprising, then, that he should be tempted by the single, irresponsible life, by the cheap thrills offered by Julie Wilder.

No. That was wrong. Julie wasn't cheap. What if her previous boyfriend was a young thug? She deserved more than a one-night stand. But not with him. It was a good thing that he and Ruth were about to go on holiday.

"No worries," Eddie told Julie and Shirley when he got back to the house. "They were harping on about an identity parade, but that bouncer won't pick me out."

"What if he does?" Shirley asked.

"The bouncer saw the car that hit him, not me. Even if he did, Satnam saw my gun and he's been to see the bouncer. They both know what'd happen if –" Eddie grimaced, then laughed, leaving the rest of the sentence unsaid.

"Is there anything else?" Shirley wanted to know.

"What do you mean?"

"Anything else they could have a witness for? To run a parade."

The word "parade" was funny, Julie thought: made it sound like Eddie was going to a celebration, or a show.

"They were asking about Friday night," he told them. "I might need to cover my tracks there. Any chance that I could have been here with you?"

"Afraid not," Shirley said. "Three police came round, after I belted Curt. They'd have seen you."

"Pity."

"When *were* you here?" Shirley went on. "Just in case they ask."

"Before tonight? Tuesday night and Wednesday, but not Thursday. Make sure you're definite about Wednesday."

"Any particular reason?" Julie asked, speaking for the first time. She hadn't told Ben Shipman that there'd been anyone visiting on Tuesday and Wednesday. She considered telling Eddie this now, but decided it might put him in an even worse temper.

"Never you mind," Eddie said. "Where's that Scotch? I told you I'd be back to finish it."

14

Every week, despite having won the jackpot once, Gordon Loscoe sat down to watch the National Lottery draw. Natalie couldn't understand why he bought even the one ticket. Not only that, but her dad still played the same numbers each time, the ones he'd won with: 12, 17, 31, 42, 46 and 49. It was a fourteen-million-to-one chance that they'd win once, but how could they possibly win again? Dad said that they were as likely to win a second time as anybody else. Natalie didn't believe him. But then, neither of them were any good at maths.

She'd worked on Mum and bought a leather skirt like the one she'd tried to nick, promising only that she'd not put it on until she'd said goodnight to Dad. Now she had on a halter top over denim jeans with her navel showing between.

"Who you going out with tonight?" Dad asked.

"Me mates."

"What mates?"

Natalie hardly had any friends from the Maynard Estate days. And, though there were a couple of girls she hung around with at school, they weren't the sort you'd go out with on a Saturday night. Nevertheless, she threw their names at Dad.

"Saskia. Emily."

"Whose house?"

"Emily's."

"Oh, yeah. I see her dad down the golf club. Big producer at Central. Say hello for me."

"If he's in."

"You not staying to watch the numbers?"

She shook her head. The programme began. The doorbell rang.

"See who that is on your way out," Dad ordered.

Natalie went to the door, working out her moves. She'd have to let whoever it was in, pretend to go out, then sneak back inside for the skirt, before walking down to the bus stop. She checked the security hole. There was a car in the drive, a grey Merc. How had that got in, when the security gates were shut? Then Natalie recognized the bloke standing on the porch: Eddie Broom. Uncle Eddie, she called him when she was a kid. She'd known he'd show up sooner or later. Dad must have known too. She opened the door.

"Natalie!" he said. "My pearl. You're looking gorgeous tonight. How old are you now? Sixteen?"

"Fourteen," she told him.

"Never! Then I can still give you a kiss." He leant over and embraced her in a clumsy hug. His breath smelt of whisky. Natalie felt something cold and metallic against her bare midriff. Maybe it was the belt buckle of his trousers. "You be careful going out for the evening dressed like that. There are fellas who'd be all over a girl like you."

Natalie smiled shyly. Good thing he hadn't seen her in the leather skirt.

"I know, Uncle Eddie," she told him. "Don't worry. We grow up quicker than in your day."

Let him make of that what he will.

"I'm after your father."

"He's in the lounge, watching the box."

"And your mother?"

She'd drunk herself all the way inside a gin bottle, as usual. "She's upstairs, having a rest."

"All right. I'll see myself in. You have a good night, Natalie."

"Who is it?" Dad called from the lounge.

Eddie didn't reply.

"G'night," Natalie said. She went out the front door, then walked round to the conservatory, where she'd left the skirt. Next, instead of slipping the skirt on, she went through the dining room, up to the lounge door, and listened.

*   *   *

"I don't want to watch," Clare said. "I'm getting changed."

"So am I," Ruth told her, "but come on. You might as well."

Reluctantly, Clare followed Ruth downstairs. To her surprise, kd lang, a singer she liked, was performing on the Lottery show. She let herself enjoy the song, but was irritated by the blather afterwards about the good causes the Lottery supported. Earlier in the day, she'd been at Mum and Dad's for a delayed birthday meal. They'd tried to be cheerful, but it was clear that the bank was on the point of calling in Dad's overdraft. He could go bust. Some of the money from the Lottery went on building works, sure. But it all went to the big firms, not people like Dad. Those who had, got more. Those who didn't got trampled on. That was the way things worked, everywhere.

Gary was visiting a friend, and would be back later. The three women sat in the large, knocked-through living room, watching Sam's big, old TV set. At last, the numbers came up. Between them, they had ten sets to follow.

"All these numbers," Sam said. "It's like being at bingo."

"Don't tell us you do bingo!" Ruth said, sarkily.

"I've been a couple of times, with a mate. It was a laugh, all women together. But they've closed the place down now. Lottery took away too much trade."

The first ball came down. 3. None of them had it.

"There goes the jackpot," Ruth said.

Next, 17. Clare had this on two of her tickets. No one else did. The next number was 49. This was one of Sam's. She cheered loudly.

Next was 42. No one had that, either.

It was followed by 31. Clare had this, on the same card as one of the 17s. If she got another number, she stood to make £10, a £2 profit on the CID officers' £8 outlay.

The final number was 12. Clare had this, but not on the same ticket as the 31 and 17.

"Turn it off," Sam said.

The bonus-ball number only counted if you had five of the first six right.

"What was your best one?" Ruth asked. "Two numbers?"

Clare nodded.

"I didn't get any."

"One," Sam said, tearing up her ticket. "Better than last week."

"Complete waste of time," Clare said, throwing her tickets in the bin. "And money."

The three women went back upstairs to get ready to go out.

"Congratulations," Eddie said to Dad. "Five

numbers. You won."

Dad was laughing, pouring them drinks, but his nervousness showed in the loudness of his laugh.

Natalie had been excited, listening to the numbers. It reminded her of that night, nearly two years ago, when they really did win, and the world became magic. In those days, the three of them watched the show together, as a family. When the sixth number came up, they all hugged, then pinched each other, to make sure that they weren't dreaming.

"What's five numbers worth then?" Eddie asked. "A thousand, a thousand five?"

"Something like that."

"A little bird tells me you dump at least twice that much, most nights, down the casino."

Dad said nothing. Natalie wondered if it was true. Dad only told them about the casino when he'd won. Eddie's voice became ugly, aggressive.

"Is that why you did it, Gordon? Or were you just taking the piss?"

"You don't understand," Dad said. "Believe it or not, I needed the money."

"I understand that, all right," Eddie told him. "What I don't understand is why you didn't come to me in the first place. We were always mates, weren't we? I trusted you. You're about the only one I did trust, outside."

Dad apologized, poured Uncle Eddie another drink. Eddie calmed down a little.

"You've put me in a difficult position," he said. "The police are asking where I was on Friday night and I don't have an alibi."

"They can't have anything," Dad told him.

"Maybe they're just fishing. But you used things I told you, in confidence."

"Nothing I couldn't have read about in the papers," Dad protested.

"I wouldn't bet on it," Eddie said, darkly. "Police are cagey about what they put in the papers. What kind of gun did you say they used?"

"Gun?" Dad asked. "I thought... I could have sworn you said it was mostly knives. Because they were quiet."

"Only when we're taking them to the machines, you stupid—"

The men were interrupted by Mum, staggering, half-awake, into the room.

"Eddie, it's been ages! How are you?"

"Not so good, Maxine. We've got a problem."

"Where are you going?" Julie asked Curt.

Mum was already out. She was meeting Uncle Eddie later, and had gone for a drink with a few mates first.

"I'm going into town. It's Saturday night."

"I know it's Saturday night. I thought you might keep me company. You've only just come out of hospital."

"'S boring at home."

"Thanks a lot."

"'S not my fault you dumped Dave."

Actually, it was, in a way, but Julie said nothing. She dug into her purse, found a couple of quid.

"Go to the offy first, get us a bottle of cider."

Curt did as she asked. He was wearing his best clothes, Julie saw. He must have got money from somewhere. Uncle Eddie, probably. He would try to get into some club or other, but he'd fail. Curt could pass as sixteen, but not eighteen, and most clubs had age limits of twenty-one in order to keep out kids like Curt. Mind you, that had never stopped Julie, not before she had Tammy.

"Have fun," she said, as he left, walking awkwardly because of the bruises concealed beneath his long-sleeved shirt.

Julie wished that she could afford a babysitter, go out herself. If Mum was a bit older, or married, she might stay home nights. But who would Mum marry? Someone like Eddie, who liked clubs and casinos? They wouldn't stay home on a Saturday night. Julie was stuck inside until she was Mum's age. Only...

Julie realized that, for the first time in eight days, she'd forgotten the Lottery money, which would pay for all the babysitting she wanted. No. Not forgotten, exactly. She had stopped believing in it. Like God, or Father Christmas, it was no longer there. She felt a sudden loss, followed by a kind of relief. Then she turned the telly back on.

Ruth, Clare and Sam treated themselves to a taxi into town. It couldn't go all the way to Barrios because of the bollards outside Oddbins, but they were only a hop and a jump from the bar. Clare wore the black dress she'd bought for the Mess Ball, four weeks before, while Ruth had on an elegant, shiny number with a silver sliver of a zip down the front. Sam, with her hair freshly highlighted, wearing a linen dress that flattered her figure, looked five years younger.

"You ought to get lucky tonight," Ruth told her.

Sam shrugged bravely. She and Ruth had had a heart-to-heart on Thursday, after Sam split up with Steve, each trying to convince the other that Sam had done the right thing. But Sam no longer seemed so sure.

"I'm not looking for anyone," she said. "The last thing I want to do is get off with a policeman."

It was just gone nine. A sign on the nightclub entrance said: "Sorry. Private Party Tonite". The security bloke nodded at the girls as they went in.

"I don't know why you hired him," Sam said. "I mean, who's going to try and gatecrash a party full of police officers?"

"Don't harp on about it all being police," Clare said. "There are other people, too. And no one's in uniform, so how would a gatecrasher know?"

"It's not that we'd have trouble throwing people out," Ruth told Sam. "More that we don't want the embarrassment in the first place."

Sam nodded. Anyway, there wasn't much likelihood of gatecrashers. The nightclub entrance was closed, and you had to go through a side alley and a small courtyard to get to Barrio's. They'd booked both bar and club. A separate stairway at the side of the bar led downstairs to the dancing.

The night was still warm, and a couple of people were drinking in the courtyard. Clare said hello to them, and stayed to talk. They must be old friends from school, Ruth guessed. She and Sam climbed the stairs to the airy wine bar. A few people had arrived. Ben wasn't among them. Paul Grace waved, and made a gesture as if to ask where Clare was. Sam pointed back down the stairs. Ruth ordered two Bacardi and Cokes.

"Let me get that," Paul insisted. "You both look ravishing," he went on.

"Wait till you see Clare," Ruth told him, enjoying the compliment.

Clare was coming up the stairs now. Paul went over to her and they kissed, like lovers meeting after a long absence, the Inspector lifting Clare off the ground. From a distance, in the badly lit bar, he looked the younger of the two.

More guests arrived. Many were in the job, and

knew both Clare and Grace, but not that they were in a relationship. As the couple stood, greeting newcomers with their arms around each other, eyes popped out of heads. Ruth enjoyed the spectacle. Here was the youngest Inspector in the country pairing off with the prettiest PC. There would be plenty of gossip on Monday. Ruth wondered what would happen when Neil showed up. She also wondered where Ben was. She wanted tonight to go perfectly for both of them. The lunch with his parents had been strained, awkward. Ben's mum and dad had been pleasant to Ruth, but it was obvious that they couldn't understand what their son was doing with her. The nicer they were, the more embarrassed Ruth had felt. She'd invented an excuse for them to leave early, and neither she nor Ben had mentioned the lunch since.

Below the bar, the DJ finished setting up. Dance music began, but no one went downstairs yet. More people arrived. The party would soon be in full swing. Ruth kept turning down drinks, chatting with people she barely knew. Background music was piped through upstairs. Clare and Paul started to do a soft-shoe shuffle to the Cure's "Love Cats". Someone wanted to propose a toast, but Ruth made them wait. She wanted Ben there. Where was he? He couldn't desert her now. They were going on holiday tomorrow. It was her birthday party and it wasn't like Ben to be late. Where was he?

15

It was one thing, sneaking into town by yourself on a Saturday night. It was another, finding something to do once you got there. Natalie was turned down at the door of Fat Sam's bar as soon as she got off the bus. However, there weren't any bouncers on the pub doors this early in the evening. She could get in, but not get served. Natalie could pass as sixteen, but never eighteen.

She tried the Bluebell, the Old Angel and the Newmarket. No joy. Anyway, what would she do if she did get served, sit around and wait to be chatted up? It felt cheap, or silly, or both. To do that kind of thing, you needed to be with a gang of girls. Natalie didn't have a gang, not any more.

She'd heard older girls talking at school. They

reckoned that the best thing to do was this: go into a place that was full of young blokes on the make, hang around like you were waiting for someone, then let one of them buy you a drink. If you liked him, then you went off somewhere else with him, pretending that you were standing the other bloke up. If things went badly, you pretended that your date had arrived, and cleared off, sharpish.

Natalie decided that she might as well go the whole hog, and walked into Jacey's, which was a cross between a wine bar and a pub. People went there before the clubs. But she'd arrived too early. It was busy, but not busy enough to camouflage her. There was no one else who looked a day under seventeen. Natalie did a quick scan of the layout. She was about to head for a side room when an amiable-looking bloke called to her from behind the bar.

"Find somewhere else to drink, love. Don't make me throw you out."

Humiliated, Natalie turned tail and hurried back to the Market Square. Sod it. She'd go to the pictures.

Yet when she looked at what was showing at the Odeon and MGM, the only things she fancied were 18 certificates. Natalie wasn't going to risk another embarrassment. She walked up Market Street, looking in the record-shop windows, wondering whether her dad and Eddie had gone out yet, in which case she might go home. She turned on to Lower Parliament Street. There was nothing along here except for a wine bar that she wouldn't even risk going into. Oh, and across the street was an amusement arcade. She'd been thrown out of it a couple of times when she was twelve. Now, however, Natalie was officially old enough to go in: fourteen. Not that there was much reason to. When he won the Lottery, Dad bought Natalie every kind of game that she could want: a Playstation, Nintendo, a PC with all the latest software. She'd gorged on it for a while, but, somehow, it wasn't the same as being in an arcade, paying money. So she only used the PC for homework, and the games were shoved away under her bed.

Natalie crossed the road at the pedestrian lights, turned right and went in, wondering if she could recapture any of the fun she used to have. If Dad was telling Eddie the truth, and he was nearly broke, maybe she'd have to get used to cheap thrills again. But the arcade had changed. It had a new door and carpet. The inside was a lot smarter, and there were no games as such, only fruit machines.

"Hey, Natalie, isn't it? You still at Rushcliffe?"

Natalie recognized the boy: Curt Wilder. His dad used to. be a friend of her dad, but he'd always ignored her when they were at the same school, back when she was in year seven and he was in year eight. Then he'd got expelled, or suspended for something or other, just before Dad bought that winning ticket.

"No. I moved."

"Me too. I heard about … you know. So what are you doing here?"

"I was supposed to meet some mates," Natalie told him. "They didn't show up."

"Same here."

He didn't believe her and she didn't believe him. Which was all right. It made them equal. Back when they were at Rushcliffe, Natalie was a bit scared of Curt. He had a wild reputation. He still looked like a rough boy, but there was something desirable about him, something sweet and vulnerable, like he'd just lost a fight.

"You like it here?" she asked.

"'S crap. You got much money?"

"Plenty."

"Fancy going to that virtual reality place?"

"Sure," Natalie said. Her dad had taken her there a couple of times. It was expensive, but a lot of fun if you were with someone. "Why not?"

They walked out into the evening, the youngest couple on the street. This was, Natalie decided, her first date. So what if she was paying for it?

"Where you go now?" Curt asked her.

She began to talk about school and how much she hated it. Soon they were both talking nineteen-to-the-dozen and Natalie felt a huge relief flowing over her. She was out, out, out.

*　　*　　*

"I can't understand," Neil was saying, for the third or fourth time. "A creep like Grace."

"I don't think he's a creep," Ben said. "Everyone respects him."

"I'm not saying he can't do his job. But he must be ten years older than her."

"Seven or eight, maybe. So what?"

Ben wondered how old Julie Wilder was. Not that it mattered. Age was a state of mind, he reckoned, not the number of years you'd tallied up.

"What does she see in him?"

"What does it matter?"

"You know, when she first started going out with me, I knew it was partly because she wanted to find out about a case – her brother's death. You think she's going out with Grace to get promotion?"

"Oh, come on, Neil. You know Clare better than that. Grace had her transferred to CID to save embarrassment, avoid any conflict of interest. He's a stickler for the rules."

"You don't have to tell me about it." Neil had knocked back another pint. "Same again?"

"No. We ought to get going." Neil was already well on the way to being wasted.

"I'll just get a half."

"No. Help me with this."

Ben poured most of his glass into Neil's. He didn't want too much booze to stop him having a good time tonight. He looked at his watch.

"Come on. It's nearly ten. Ruth'll be worried."

They finished their drinks and hurried down Clumber Street. As they passed the council houses, Ben noticed Curt Wilder walking towards him, hand in hand with a pretty girl. Ben looked away quickly. He didn't want to think about the Wilder family any more tonight.

No one was on the door at the club. The bouncer was inside the courtyard, chatting up a suntanned DC in a short dress. He didn't look up as Ben and Neil passed him. He didn't notice the teenage couple who followed them in, either.

"Come on, we can get in here," Curt had told Natalie.

She followed him down the alleyway, behind two blokes, unsure whether this was a good idea. The virtual reality games had been a blast and she was still on a high from them. She didn't want to spoil the high by getting thrown out of somewhere. This was the best night she'd had in ages.

"The sign says it's a private party, but you can get in from the bar up here. My sister told me all the tricks. She used to be brilliant at getting in places for free."

"Used to?" Natalie asked, as they ignored the people standing at the bottom of the stairs and charged up to the bar. She remembered Julie Wilder, one of the best-looking girls at the school when Natalie went to Rushcliffe, all the boys after her. "What happened?"

"She's got a kid now," Curt said. "Look. Food."

There were various nibbles on plates around the place. Curt swooped on them like he hadn't eaten for days. Natalie wasn't hungry, but she took some bits of salami on a stick, to be polite, looking around her as she did. Everyone looked really old, in their twenties. A few were even older than that.

"What are you kids doing here?"

The speaker was a beefy bloke with short hair, like a policeman's. Natalie nearly panicked. She tried to get Curt's attention, but he was absorbed with stuffing his face. Then she saw the big notice on the wall: *Happy 21st, Ruth and Clare!!!*

"I'm Clare's younger sister," she blurted out, unconvincingly.

"I didn't know Clare had a younger sister," the bloke told her.

Natalie fronted it out. Curt was coming to her side now.

"Well, she has. I'm her. And this is my boyfriend."

The bloke looked embarrassed. "All right, sorry. How come you kids haven't got drinks?"

"They wouldn't serve me," Curt told him, putting on a slightly pathetic voice. "All I wanted was a beer."

"Go on, then," the bloke said. "Just don't tell anyone, eh?"

He gave a huge, fake laugh.

"And what about you, darlin'?"

"Bacardi and Coke, please."

"Same tipple as your sister. Well, just this once."

As he went off, Curt looked at Natalie and it was all they could do not to crack up with laughter. The bloke got served quickly.

"So, are you thinking of following in Clare's footsteps?" he asked, as he handed Natalie her drink.

That put her on the spot. She mumbled something, hoping he'd give up.

"Pardon?"

"Not on your life," she said, assertively.

"Can't say as I blame you. It's not a great job for a woman, especially a good-looking one like you or your sister."

"We're going for a dance," Curt interrupted him.

"Sure. Have fun, kids."

They took the staircase down to the club, which, thankfully, was badly lit. The music was good, but, rather than dance, Curt found a really dark table. They didn't want anyone pointing them out to Clare, whoever she was.

"What's it like, then, winning the Lottery?" Curt shouted in her ear.

"It was great at first. But then people go funny on you. Sometimes I wish we'd never got all that money, that we were still on the estate, like you."

"You wouldn't if you were there," Curt said.

"How would you know?"

"I won the Lottery," he shouted. "Last week."

Natalie thought he was having a joke with her.

"Then how come I paid for the Virtual Reality Centre?"

"Haven't had the cheque yet. Fifty grand. So, next time, I'll treat you. You know, if you want a —"

"Next time?" Natalie smiled at him. "Sure. I do."

That would have been a good point for him to kiss her, but he didn't. Curt was too shy, Natalie thought. But he wasn't bad-looking. With some better clothes, he'd be more than presentable.

"Hold on," she said. "How could you win? You're not old enough."

"Can you keep a secret?" Curt shouted.

Gary arrived at the party, waving his Lottery ticket around.

"I won a tenner!" he announced. "Second time this year."

He joined Clare, Paul and Sam, dancing to Underworld. Gary was a good dancer. Clare and Paul, however, were tiring, so they took a break just as Chris Dylan, drunk and unco-ordinated, hit the dance floor. Sam must be a little gone, Clare thought. Otherwise, why would she be letting Chris take her hand and throw her around like that?

"She's too good for him," Paul said.

"I know. But I feel sorry for Chris. He's just had a messy divorce."

The Sergeant waved at them and shouted.

"Just bought your sister a drink. She's a looker, just like you. That leather skirt—"

"My sister?" Clare queried, thinking he was even drunker than he looked.

"Sitting over there, with her boyfriend. Not sure about him, mind."

"Oh. Right. Thanks."

As Chris returned to the dance floor, Clare looked where he had pointed. There, sitting in the darkest corner of the club, was Natalie Loscoe. She recognized the boy with her, too.

"I don't believe it!" she said to Paul. "Look."

"How did they get in here?"

"I don't suppose they know what this is."

They talked over what to do.

"Let's go and surprise them," Paul suggested.

"Better, why don't we sit down next to them and see how long it takes them to notice?"

"Right," Paul said.

He laughed, but then his expression became more thoughtful.

"You never know," he added. "We might find out something."

"So we put it in my sister's name. No one can prove she didn't buy it."

"What about the bloke who sold you the ticket?"

Curt looked a little shifty. He muttered something

172

that sounded like, "We squared him," and Natalie decided not to pursue it.

"Can you keep a secret?" she asked.

"Better than anyone."

"My dad's spent all the money. You hear about the burglary we had?"

"The motorway team, yeah."

"It wasn't the motorway team."

A couple had sat down near them, so Natalie leant over and spoke right into Curt's ear.

"It was a fake, for the insurance. Mum and me, we both had to do this big act, like we'd been robbed. Dad told us exactly what to say."

Curt had a good laugh.

"That's brilliant! And you got away with it?"

Natalie shushed him and kept talking in his ear.

"Think so. Only thing is, this old mate of Dad's – Eddie – he knows what's going on. You see –"

"Eddie?" Curt said. "You don't mean Eddie Broom, do you?"

"That's right," Natalie told him, moving back to look at Curt, and being forced to shout again. "I call him Uncle Eddie."

"Me too. He's staying with us at the moment."

Natalie swore. "It's a small world, isn't it?"

A hand came down on Curt's shoulder and they both looked up. It was the Inspector, the one who'd come to the house on the night of the fake burglary.

"You're right," he said. "It *is* a small world."

16

Paul Grace enjoyed the way the kids' expressions changed from animation to sheer disbelief. He was sitting nearest to them, so had heard most of their conversation. Now he didn't know what to do. The last thing he wanted on a night like this was to get tied up in police work. Who was the on-call CID officer? Practically everyone involved with the Loscoe burglary was at the party tonight.

But he had to do something. The Wilder kid looked like he would do a runner any minute.

"Did you realize," Clare was asking him, "that this is a police do?"

The kids sat there, too embarrassed to reply. Paul leant over them.

"Don't move," he said. "I'm going to sort this

out, but if you try to scarper, there'll be real trouble."

Leaving Clare to keep an eye on them, Paul looked around for John Greasby. The two men were equals, but it was the older man's case. He found the DI in the upstairs bar, nursing a large scotch, and told him what he'd heard. John Greasby swore.

"I was sure that the Loscoe robbery was the real thing."

"What do you want to do about them?"

"I can't deal with this now," John said. "I've had too many. And the on-call's a bloke from Hucknall. He won't know a thing about the case."

"We can't just let it go," Paul told him.

"You're sober, aren't you?"

"Yes. I'm driving."

Greasby thought for a moment.

"Take the kids over to the station, question them, and have a uniform take them home. You'll be back inside the hour."

Paul objected. "We're not supposed to question kids under sixteen without a suitable adult present. And, from the sound of it, all three parents are in it up to their necks."

Greasby was unimpressed. "If you're going to be a stickler for the rules, drive them home yourself, and have a chat with them on the way. No solicitor can object to that."

Paul thought it over as he went back downstairs.

The under-age Lottery ticket didn't concern him — that sort of thing happened all the time. It was a problem for the Lottery organizers, not the police. However, it sounded like the newsagent was in on it, too. Any decision on that case would have to wait. The burglary was what interested him. *Conspiracy to defraud. Wasting police time.* And why had Eddie Broom's name come up again? He wished he'd been able to hear more. But maybe he'd heard enough to bluff it out.

He told Clare what he wanted to do.

"You don't mind?"

She gave him one of her big, sexy smiles.

"I'd mind if you didn't. I'd come with you, only, it is my party."

"Come on," Paul said to the teenagers. "Natalie, you'll have to squash into the back of my car while I drop off Curt first."

Julie was about to go to bed when she heard a car pull up outside. She thought it was Mum and Eddie, but when she looked through the nets, she saw a flash sports car and her brother get out of it. She ran to the door.

"Curt, are you mad? You can't nick a car like that. It's the sort everyone looks at. The police'll be round in five minutes."

"They're here already," Curt said.

A pale young man in a white shirt was sitting in

the driver's seat.

"What's he done?"

"Nothing, tonight. I was giving him a lift home. Is Mr Broom in?"

"Not back yet."

"Do you know where he is?"

Julie looked at her watch. Eddie had promised the police that he'd let them know of his whereabouts when he wasn't at home. If she didn't tell this copper, Eddie might get into trouble.

"He's with Mum, at a club, somewhere. The Black Orchid maybe. He often hits the casinos at about two."

"Which one, the Stakis, or the one in the Lace Market?"

"How would I know?"

The copper left.

"What the hell's going on?" Julie asked Curt, when the copper was gone.

Curt looked anguished.

"I've blown it. I was shooting my big mouth off and that bloke overheard."

"But we swore we wouldn't tell anyone!"

"We told Uncle Eddie, didn't we? And this girl, she's dead nice."

Julie groaned. Of course, there had to be a girl in it. She should never have let him go out.

"We're going to lose it," Curt said. "All that money. And it's my fault." He was starting to cry.

Julie held him.

"Maybe we'll lose it," Julie said, "and maybe we won't. But it doesn't matter. It was your money. You won it, so it was yours to lose. And what you've never had, you don't miss. Right?"

"Wrong," Curt said.

Julie nodded. She hadn't even convinced herself.

"Come on," she told Curt, "tell me about this nice girl."

The party was beginning to wear on Ruth. She liked dancing, but her feet were tired, and she'd had enough of shouting conversations with drunks. Ben seemed to feel the same way. They left the dance-floor and went back upstairs. By the bar, Sam was trying to fend off Chris Dylan. The crowd had thinned. Clare was talking to a couple whom Ruth didn't know. Ruth found it odd, seeing all these people from Clare's past, old friends whom she hardly saw any more. Ruth hadn't invited any of her friends from Halifax. When she joined the police force, she'd put her old life behind her. Now she realized how much the job had taken over both their lives. Ruth went to say goodbye to Clare.

"Where's Paul?" she asked.

"Not here. It's a long story. He'll be back."

"Ben and I are off. We want to be bright-eyed and bushy-tailed for our flight tomorrow."

"Fine. You might want to take Sam with you."

"We're going to Ben's," Ruth objected. "Gary could take her."

"You don't have to tell Chris Dylan that. She looks like she needs to be rescued."

"All right. And, if I don't see you in the morning –"

Clare gave Ruth a smug, happy smile.

"Who knows where I'll sleep tonight," she said. "Have a great holiday. I wish I was having one."

Ruth managed to wrest Sam from the drunken DS. The three of them walked to the Market Square and queued for a taxi. The night was still young and the queue wasn't long. Sam began to talk to herself.

"I should have stayed with Steve," she said. "Why throw away a good thing? You should have seen his face when I told him."

"It's not too late to change your mind," Ruth told her, but Sam wasn't listening.

"'I'm too old,' I told him. 'You're better off without me. We don't have a future, and, if we don't finish soon, I'm going to end up getting hurt.' But now I *am* hurt."

They got into the taxi, and dropped Sam off in Forest Fields first. Ruth went in with her and collected her bags. They were taking a taxi to East Midlands Airport in the morning.

"Why were you really so late?" Ruth asked, when they were in Ben's flat.

"Neil. He was a bit cut up about Clare going out

with the boss."

"He's no right. I've seen his new girlfriend. She's a looker."

"She is. But, you know, he went out with Clare for two years. And I may be wrong, because it's not exactly the sort of thing blokes tell each other…"

"What?" Ruth asked, intrigued.

"I think there's a certain amount of sexual jealousy in the equation. Neil reckons the Inspector might be getting something that he never did."

"Clare once told me," Ruth revealed, "that she thought the next person she slept with would be the person she married."

"Really?" Ben said. "So the Inspector's got no chance?"

Ruth smiled and cuddled up to him.

"I didn't say that. Clare's being quite cagey about how she feels."

They kissed.

"But it wouldn't surprise me," Ruth went on, "if, by the time we get back, Clare and Paul have got themselves engaged."

17

Natalie would never have guessed that the night would end like this, with her sitting in the front of a smart sports car, being driven home by a good-looking bloke. But there, the fantasy ended. The bloke was a police inspector and he was asking her uncomfortable questions.

"Did your mother tie you up, or was it your father?"

Natalie didn't answer. Actually, she'd refused to be tied up. Then, when Dad got back from the casino, he'd insisted on her being tied up for a few minutes, to make sure that there were marks on her arms.

"And, if your dad was at the casino, how did your Mum manage to get to the Asda car park?"

Mum had a mate who lived on Noel St, next to Asda. Dad had dropped her off on the way to the casino and she'd hidden at the friend's house. Unfortunately, the friend's boyfriend had got a bit carried away when Mum asked him to give her a knock on the head. But Natalie said none of this. She kept quiet.

"She didn't give herself that nasty cut on the head, did she?"

"You'll have to ask her."

"Oh, come on, Natalie. You were there."

Flustered, Natalie tried to backtrack.

"That story, the one I told Curt, I made it up. There wasn't a word of truth in it. I was trying to impress him."

She wondered how much the Inspector had really heard.

"Forget it, Natalie. What you said fitted with everything we've found out in our investigation. Where's your father tonight?"

"I don't know."

"Where was he when you went out?"

"Home."

"Alone?"

"Eh?"

"You told Curt that Eddie was there."

Had she? Natalie didn't remember telling Curt that, but she must have, if the Inspector had overheard it.

"Yes. And Mum."

"Why did Eddie come round, Natalie?"

They weren't far from the house now. Mum would be worried about her. If she was conscious, that was. Mum could handle these questions. Why should Natalie? She never wanted to get involved in the first place.

"Were Eddie and your father arguing, Natalie?"

"They might have been."

"Come on, you can do better than that."

How much did he know? Natalie was tired. She wasn't sure about anything any more.

"Ask them. All right?"

"No. You overheard their conversation. What were they arguing about? Tell me. Come on, Natalie, what difference does it make? I know that you faked the burglary. You might as well tell me the rest."

"Uncle Eddie said Dad could get him into a lot of trouble," Natalie said. "He was mad at Dad because of something to do with the burglary."

"You'll have to be more precise."

"I can't!" Natalie protested, getting upset. "That's all I know."

It was the truth, near enough. She had her suspicions, but, in a family like hers, you tried to know as little as possible.

"Have you got a card for this?" the Inspector asked.

They were at the security gate.

"No. But it's all right. There's a side door I can go through. Thanks for the ride."

She started to unbuckle her seat belt.

"Not so fast."

She stopped.

"I'm coming with you, Natalie. You can make this hard, or easy. Tell me what I want to know, and your parents won't have to realize that you blurted it all out in a conversation with your boyfriend in a club full of policemen."

Natalie panicked.

"You mustn't tell them about Curt! They'd kill me."

Even two years ago, Curt had had a reputation on the Maynard Estate. If Dad didn't take it seriously, Mum would, and she would be grounded until she was sixteen.

"Then tell me what I want to know."

Natalie thought. They already had practically all of it. What harm was there?

"All right," she said. "You're right. Dad faked the robbery. He told me it was for a laugh, to swindle the insurance. He'd bought some right rubbish when we first won the money and he wanted shot of it. He spent the week before the robbery taking bits and pieces from the house and dumping them on the tip, or in the Trent. I heard him and Mum talking – he bought a lot of stuff lately and sold even more, 'cos he knew he was going to claim it on the insurance."

"But you think he's really short of money?"

"That's what Eddie said. But Eddie was mad about something else. I don't understand it all. Eddie said Dad had made a mistake. It was guns, not knives. The motorway team only used knives in places where a gun might be heard. Dad was annoyed."

"Where did Eddie get his information?" the Inspector asked.

"Newspaper, same as Dad, I guess."

"All the newspaper reports said was that the gang were armed. They didn't say what with."

"I dunno, then. Look, can I go in now, please? Don't wake my mum."

The Inspector thought about it.

"I'll walk up to the house with you."

He locked the car and came through the side door with Natalie. Once they got around the corner, they saw that the house was dark.

"Can you tell if your dad's in?" Inspector Grace asked.

"He isn't. See, the garage door's open. His Porsche isn't there."

"And Eddie Broom?"

"His car's gone, too."

"All right. You go and get your beauty sleep."

"What should I tell Mum and Dad?"

"Whatever you like. You're not in trouble – not yet, anyway."

"I lied about the burglary."

"Your father told you to. I can't see us deciding to prosecute you." He smiled and added: "As for the other thing, it'd be a bit embarrassing, wouldn't it, arresting you for under-age drinking at a police birthday party."

"Will you be coming for Mum and Dad?"

"We might question them on Monday," the Inspector said, casually. They were at the door. Natalie muttered a goodnight before going inside, and straight to bed. How much longer, she wondered, would they live in this big house? Maybe they could move back to the Meadows, and she could live near Curt.

Curt. The thought of his smile kept her warm. Natalie knew, even though she hadn't kissed him yet, that he was going to be her first boyfriend. She worried about him, though. How much had the Inspector overheard? She didn't mind giving her Dad away, but it would be a terrible, terrible disaster if Curt didn't get his money.

Paul Grace drove back into the city, but not at speed. He was working out whether he'd done the right thing. Detective work involved difficult decisions. Should he have gone in and questioned the mother? She probably knew what Eddie

Broom's secret was. But there was no point. Paul had already guessed it. The point was to get proof.

He needed to get back to Clare. She was never far from his thoughts these days. What was it with him and her? Love, or lust, or both? He didn't know. Passion could play tricks on the mind. Sometimes, you only found out how you really felt about someone after you'd slept with them. It had happened to Paul before. He would pursue a woman, thinking that he was falling in love. Finally, he got her. Then, one day, he would wake up to find himself next to an average woman with an average brain, average ambitions and a beautiful body. Finally, even the beauty became boring, and he broke it off.

Paul parked at the back of the club and went to look for Clare. By Monday, Eddie Broom and Gordon Loscoe would have worked out how close the police were. Maybe Eddie would skip the area, rather than face the identity parade. It made sense to pick him up tonight, if they could. But Paul didn't want to go collecting criminals. He wanted to go home with Clare.

His girlfriend was upstairs in the bar when he got back to the party, drinking coffee. At the table were John Greasby and Tracey Bradford from CID, together with Gary Monk, from Paul's shift.

"You took your time," Clare said. "They're about to throw us out."

"Any result?" John Greasby asked.

"One definite. One possible."

"Come on, then," Clare said. "Tell us."

Paul summed up what he had found out.

"Where do you reckon they are now?" Greasby asked, when he'd finished.

"Casino," Paul said. "Generally, Loscoe stays there until at least three."

"And Broom?"

"Probably with him. Or out with Shirley Wilder."

Greasby nodded.

"It'd make sense to pick up at least one of them tonight, so they can't concoct a story together when they realize we're on to them."

"It better be Loscoe," Paul said. "We've got something definite on him."

Greasby nodded. "Why don't you call a couple of uniforms, for back-up?"

"On a Saturday night? It's chaos out there."

"West Bridgford'll find someone for you."

The waiters were turning off lights. Paul felt like the victim of a sick joke. He was being manoeuvred into working all night, simply because he was the only one there who wasn't plastered. He'd brought the car because he wanted to take Clare home in it, not to ferry around under-age fraudsters.

"That taxi queue'll be getting big," Gary was saying to Clare. "Maybe we should walk."

"You walk," she said to Gary. "I'm going with Paul."

He looked at her.

"Are you sure?"

Her smile was full of promise.

"I'm sure."

John Greasby and Tracey Bradford left, Paul promising to ring the DI in the morning to bring him up to date. Using the phone behind the bar, he asked West Bridgford to have a car parked near the casino.

"How are we going to play this?" Clare asked, as they walked down into the dark, empty courtyard, the last to leave.

"I don't know," Paul said. "But there's something I've been wanting to do all night."

They embraced for a long time, murmuring endearments to each other.

"Sod it," Paul said, when they eventually pulled apart. "Let's just go home. It's not even my case."

"But it is mine," Clare told him. "Come on. I really want to make this a birthday to remember."

18

A police panda was waiting around the corner from the casino, with two officers inside. There was no back exit from the casino or its car park, only a sheer drop on to the small housing estate tucked away below. Paul signed them in.

"What if they're at a different one?" Clare asked Paul, as they walked up to the gaming rooms.

"This is the one that Gordon uses the most. That's them. Over there." Gordon Loscoe and Eddie Broom were sitting at the table that Gordon had been on the last time Clare was there. Paul and Clare walked over to it. As they watched, Shirley Wilder came out of the powder room and spoke to Eddie.

"Can we go now?" Clare heard her ask.

"A few minutes," he replied.

"Should we arrest Gordon now?" Clare asked Paul.

"No. Let's see what happens."

Clare hid her face behind her hair and turned to Paul.

"What if they recognize us?"

"They won't. We're not in uniform. Don't turn round, but Gordon Loscoe's leering at you. It's not a policewoman he's seeing."

Clare had only met Gordon Loscoe once, late at night, and Neil had done the talking when they were at Shirley's on Thursday. Maybe Paul was right. Out of uniform, the gamblers wouldn't recognize them. But there was always a risk.

Paul bought chips and the evening took on an air of unreality. Here Clare was, at 2.30am, sitting next to two criminals and being asked to choose a number, any number.

"Thirty-two."

Eddie Broom bet on 12, Gordon Loscoe on 15. The wheel spun.

"Eleven."

Broom and Loscoe put more chips on the same numbers as before.

"I think we should bet on this one, don't you?" Paul said, moving a small pile of chips on to 21.

"Sure," Clare said. "It worked before. Why not?"

The wheel spun. Clare watched the ball, her own

head spinning. How had she ended up here? This was a mad thing to be doing on her birthday. She didn't believe in gambling. Though that seemed silly, at this moment. Maybe everyone had the right to go mad, now and then. The wheel slowed down. Gambling, Clare decided, was only a form of recreation, or relaxation, as Paul said. True, people became addicted to it, but people could get addicted to anything: cars, cigarettes, sex, chocolate biscuits –

"Twenty-one!"

Paul whooped with delight. A big pile of chips was pushed their way.

"That's me done," Eddie Broom said.

"One more," Gordon Loscoe suggested.

He still had a couple of chips left, but Broom was already on the way to cash in his.

"Going so soon?" the manager asked Paul as he and Clare followed the other three out.

"Always quit when you're ahead."

Paul was getting edgy, Clare could see. He whispered to Clare: "Get out before them. Tell the boys in the car to wait until Loscoe's left the car park before picking him up. Then we can do him for driving under the influence. Here, take my keys. I'll meet you outside."

Clare went out and gave the waiting officers Paul's instructions, then got into Paul's Mazda. Gordon Loscoe walked straight past her and got into his Porsche. Eddie Broom and Shirley Wilder spoke to him for a few seconds, then walked over to Broom's Mercedes. As Loscoe started his engine, Paul got into the driver's seat.

"Open your handbag."

He poured in all their chips.

"I didn't have time to cash these. We'll have to make a return visit." He started the engine.

"What are we—?" Clare started to ask.

Paul shushed her.

"We need to see who leaves first."

It was Loscoe. A moment later, the Mercedes followed him. Paul switched on his lights and followed the car out. As they turned the corner on to Barker Gate, Clare saw Gordon Loscoe getting out of his car. He was clumsily parked behind the police Panda. Eddie Broom took one look, and drove on.

"Not helping his mate out," Paul said. "Very sad."

"Maybe he's over the limit himself," Clare commented.

"I doubt it. From what I've seen, Eddie's a careful man."

They followed Broom as he drove towards the Meadows. Paul did a detour, so that it didn't look like he was going to the Maynard Estate, doubling back on himself to make sure that the Mercedes was parked outside the Wilder house.

"What now?" Clare asked.

Were they going to try and arrest him here, now?

"We go home," Paul said.

"But what about –"

"Gordon Loscoe's out of the way. He won't be released until I say so. Therefore, he can't find out what Natalie told me and won't get to tell Eddie that we might be on to him."

"But Curt –"

"Curt doesn't know we're on to Eddie, only that we overheard about Gordon."

"And Natalie?"

"There's a risk that Natalie will call Curt and let him know that I was asking about Eddie, but I doubt it. Both kids are too embarrassed. She'll pretend that she didn't say anything."

Clare worked it out aloud.

"So, tomorrow, Gordon Loscoe will be expecting to be released on the drink-driving beef, and we'll start questioning him about the fake robbery instead."

"That's right. Meanwhile, Eddie will think he's got a day before the identity parade, but we'll pick him up early, before Gordon's released."

"And hope to catch him out. You should be in CID."

Paul smiled and began to drive.

"I'm heading back towards my place. Is that all right?"

"Fine," Clare told him. "You know, I'm really impressed."

"Don't be. All I'm doing is organizing the logistics. The real trick will be to get Eddie Broom to incriminate himself and give up the rest of the motorway team."

"You mean, if Candia Arnold doesn't identify him?"

"There's only a one-in-three chance of that. And Eddie doesn't seem worried about the identity parade. If Candia Arnold had seen his face, Eddie wouldn't be sticking around here. He's a dab hand at disappearing."

They reached Paul's house, and embraced as soon as they were inside the door. Tonight, Clare had no doubts. Everything felt right.

"Do you want a drink?" Paul asked, when they'd finished kissing.

"No. I've had enough. Do you have a spare toothbrush?"

He gave her one that was still in its cellophane wrapping. Clare got it open, brushed her teeth quickly, then went into the bedroom. Paul stood there in his jockey shorts.

"Don't be long," she said, as he went into the bathroom.

Paul brushed his teeth a little less thoroughly than usual, then washed his hands and face, rehearsing the contraception conversation in his head. Tonight had been a triumph. Tomorrow might, just might, be even better. But now there was only one thing on his mind. He restrained himself from running back into the room.

"Clare?"

She was lying on her side, facing him, the covers falling modestly over her chest.

"Clare?"

He thought that she was having him on. After all, he'd only been gone a couple of minutes.

"Clare. Wake up!"

She didn't respond at all, not even when he leant down and gently kissed her, not when he got into bed beside her and turned off the light. Even when he held her, as he had dreamt of holding her for months now, Clare didn't stir.

Paul lay like this for a long time, listening to Clare breathe, feeling the warmth of her body beside him, wondering what time she would wake in the morning.

19

Neil was woken by a phone call from Melanie. She was coming back to Nottingham a day early, she told him, and would be there when he got home on Friday. "I wondered, if you've got time, could you call in at some flat agencies, see if there's anywhere for me to see at the weekend?"

"Sure."

It was daft, Neil thought. Melanie couldn't afford a decent place on her own and hadn't found anyone to share with. But there was a spare room at Neil's house. There was no way that her parents would wear her living with him, Melanie said, except as a temporary measure. Fair enough. But temporary measures sometimes had a habit of becoming permanent.

The next phone call got Neil out of the shower. It

was his boss, DI Greasby.

"You left early last night, missed some interesting events."

"Did I?"

"I'll tell you all about it when you come in. I wanted Chris Dylan, but he's not answering his phone. We have Gordon Loscoe waiting for interrogation. You can back me up."

Neil dressed and drove in as quickly as he could. On the radio news, it said that a bus driver from Bolsover was the sole winner of last night's nine-million-pound National Lottery jackpot. He'd gone to work today as usual, but only to hand in his resignation. Neil wondered on what grounds Nottingham's millionaire winner had been arrested.

As it turned out, Gordon Loscoe had the same question. "Look, I'll pay the fine and lose my licence for a year, but I don't see why you had to keep me banged up overnight."

"You were well over the limit," DI Greasby pointed out.

"Yeah, but the thing is, I'm used to alcohol. It doesn't affect me. Not that I blame you lot for doing your job but –"

But. But. But. Everyone had an excuse, or a sob story. Neil waited for the Inspector to begin his ploy.

"We do have some news for you."

"What?"

"About your robbery."

"Oh. That. I don't suppose you've recovered anything? Insurance won't tell me when they're likely to pay up."

"It seems that you were right, Mr Loscoe. One of your friends was behind the burglary and kidnap."

Loscoe looked surprised.

"What? Someone on that list I gave you?"

"Not quite. Someone you must have left off by accident. Eddie Broom."

"Eddie? But –"

"You trusted him, I'm sure. However, there's evidence linking him to a number of the motorway-team burglaries. And Eddie has been an occasional visitor to your house, which would explain how the team knew which goods to take, and were able to act so quickly."

"This is nonsense. Eddie's a mate. He's a wealthy man. He doesn't need –"

"What is it that Eddie does for a living, precisely?"

"Well, I … um…"

Greasby smiled. "Eddie made a classic mistake, the night he burgled your house. He didn't give himself an alibi. Now, I want to go over those events with you again."

"*Again?* Look, I'm fed up of this. I mean, are you going to finally charge me with the drink driving and let me go? Because if you're not, then I think it's time to call my solicitor."

"That is, of course, your right," Greasby told him, "though I doubt that he'll welcome being called away from his game of golf. Why don't you take a few minutes to think it over?"

They suspended the interview and left Loscoe to stew.

"What next?" Neil asked, back in the CID office.

"I'm going to sort out this identity parade. Where's Clare? I thought she'd be in by now."

"It was a big night," Neil said. "I'll call her."

Neil dialled the number he knew by heart. Sam answered on the fourteenth ring. It sounded like he'd got her up.

"I'll go and get her."

Clare's landlady returned a couple of minutes later. "Sorry, she's out."

"Do you mean—?"

"Any message?" Sam interrupted him.

"No. It's OK." He could guess what Sam wasn't telling him. Clare hadn't spent the night there. Neil wondered what to do. He couldn't bring himself to call Clare at Inspector Grace's home, even if he knew the number.

As it turned out, there was no need. Two minutes later, the double doors swung open and Clare walked in, wearing a tracksuit that he'd never seen on her before. There was a glow in her eyes that Neil had never seen there before, either.

"You asked me to come in?" she said to DI Greasby.

He put the phone down.

"I thought you and Neil might like to pick up Eddie Broom, say that his identity parade's been moved forward."

"Fine."

"Tell him nothing else for now. We've got a strategy going. Is Paul coming in?"

"He just dropped me off. Do you want him?"

"The strategy was his idea," Greasby commented.

Clare smiled. "He was going to the gym, but he's got my pager with him, just in case."

She turned to Neil. "Shall we go?"

Neil was odd on the way over to the Maynard Estate, hardly saying a word. He didn't mention the party, or any of last night's other events. Clare guessed that he felt funny about her spending the night with Paul Grace. She didn't see why. After she finished with him, he'd found a new girlfriend within a fortnight.

They parked next to Eddie's Mercedes. Eddie had taken Shirley to the pub for Sunday lunch, Julie told them, in a harassed voice. Curt was watching a video, but Clare could tell that he was hanging on her words.

"That ... thing," Julie went on.

"What thing?" Clare asked.

"You and that other bloke overheard Curt talking last night, about my ticket."

"Oh. That."

Julie's eyes pleaded with her.

"What are you going to do about it?"

"I don't know," Clare told her, honestly. "I expect what you did happens all the time. Normally, it wouldn't be any of our business, but what happened to the newsagent –"

"He tried to blackmail me," Julie said.

"I thought as much. Have you got the money yet?"

"They're meant to be phoning me tomorrow."

Clare looked around at the shabby room, damp on the walls, holes in the carpet. It was no place for a baby to be brought up.

"I can't make any promises," she said.

But it was in no one's interests to stop Julie getting the money. All it would mean was more paperwork, more aggro.

"Thanks," Julie told her.

Eddie Broom came quietly. When Clare wouldn't tell him who the witness was at the identity parade, he didn't press the matter.

"I'll bet it's not that bouncer," he said, jokily. "I'll need to call my solicitor."

"We'll get him for you," Neil promised. "Don't worry. The identity parade won't start without him agreeing to all the details."

"OK."

Clare suppressed a smile. Eddie didn't realize that the identity parade was the least of his problems.

"Good night?" John Greasby asked Paul Grace, a twinkle in his eye that made clear precisely what question he was asking.

Paul was cagey. He'd never been one of those blokes who boasted about sexual conquests.

"Very good. I wanted to thank you for taking Clare on. It's—"

"No problem. She's a useful addition to the team. Now, I've sent Neil to get a warrant. Ready to give Loscoe a go with me?"

Paul followed the DI into an interview room. Gordon Loscoe looked like a man who had spent the night in the cells, nursing a hangover.

"You remember Inspector Grace. He came on the night when —"

"I remember."

He looked at Grace with some confusion. Doubtless he was trying to work out where he had seen him since. It didn't seem to have occurred to him that he had been set up last night. Paul put on his most cheerful voice.

"Looks like we're finally getting some progress on your burglary, Mr Loscoe. Just a few more questions before we send you on your way."

"Good."

"Did you have any idea that your friend Eddie was linked to the motorway team?"

"No. And I don't think—"

"How did Eddie tell you he made his living?"

"Buying and selling, same as he always has. We don't talk much about—"

"Why did Eddie come to see you yesterday, Mr Loscoe?"

"He comes to see me regularly. We're old mates."

"According to your wife, it was six months since his last visit. Why do you think he came round yesterday, only a week after your burglary?"

"Coincidence."

Paul leant back on his chair and sighed.

"You must stop trying to protect your friend, Mr Loscoe. We have plenty of evidence against him. And we know exactly why he came to see you."

"Tell me, then."

"To make sure that the police, and you, weren't on to him."

"No," Loscoe said, looking increasingly uneasy.

"Did he give any other reason for coming round?"

"I told you. He doesn't need a reason. We're—"

"Old friends. You said. But you have to stop protecting him, Mr Loscoe. Because, if you carry on, we can only come to one conclusion."

"And what's that then?"

"That you and Eddie colluded in the robbery, in

order to defraud the insurance company."

Loscoe snapped. "That's crap and you know it!"

Loscoe was right. But he was starting to get worried, Paul could see. John Greasby took over.

"All we're saying is that it could look bad for you. We asked around after your arrest last night. You've been losing an awful lot of money."

This was a lie, but Loscoe swallowed it.

"I can afford my losses."

"Then there's the business with the guns."

"What guns?" Loscoe asked.

"Precisely. Why was yours the one motorway-team robbery where firearms weren't used?"

"I don't know."

"Then I'll tell you," Greasby said. "You and Eddie were in on it together. You didn't want your wife and daughter scared more than was necessary."

Loscoe was silent. Paul enjoyed the way Greasby skirted round the real situation, where Maxine and Natalie were involved. A man might give up his friend to protect his wife and daughter.

The two of them pressed the question, again and again.

"All right," Gordon Loscoe said, eventually. "I can see what you're getting at. Thing is, I suppose Eddie could have been behind the robbery. He'd know where to look, and everything, like you said. And if he's in this team – which I didn't know about, God's honest truth – maybe he got a little tempted, knew that I was covered by the insurance, but – and I want to make this completely clear – I had nothing to do with it."

"Of course not," Greasby said.

"Can I go now?"

"A few more minutes."

"Is he in there?" Greasby asked Clare.

"Yes. He's already brought up solicitors."

"Get on to Birmingham, will you? Make sure that Ms Arnold's returned."

Clare did that, then observed the DI interviewing Eddie Broom. Paul sat out the interview, as Eddie might have noticed him in the casino. If he saw Paul again today, he might realize that the police knew more than they were letting on. Greasby began the questioning.

"Why did you go and see Gordon Loscoe a week after he was burgled?"

"To be sympathetic. We're mates."

"That's not what Gordon says."

Broom shrugged this off.

"If you're going to start playing me and Gordon off against each other, I want my solicitor."

"Any time," Greasby said. "Interview suspended at one-twelve pm."

He clicked the tape off and started to get up.

"Oh," he said, reaching into his pocket. "Before I go, you might like to hear this."

He put on the tape of Gordon Loscoe recorded a

few minutes earlier.

"*I suppose Eddie could have been behind the robbery. He'd know where to look, and everything, like you said. And if he's in this team — which I didn't know about, God's honest truth — maybe he got a little tempted, knew that I was covered by the insurance, but — and I want to make this completely clear — I had nothing to do with it.*"

Eddie began swearing. Greasby took the tape out and began recording again. "What's the problem? I thought you two were good mates?"

Eddie swore some more. He was completely thrown.

"Do you have an alibi for that night, Eddie?"

"I didn't do it. That half-wit Gordon did it himself. The wife and daughter were part of it. He always was a greedy bastard, Loscoe, took stupid risks. I went down for him once. Well, I'm not going down this time."

"Then you'd better prove your accusation."

Eddie stopped. He'd let off hot air, and now his brain was beginning to work again.

"I thought I said I wanted a solicitor."

"Interview suspended at one-seventeen pm."

Back in the office, Neil had come back with the warrant. Clare didn't know what it was for.

"No problem," Neil told DI Greasby.

"All right," the Detective Inspector said, with mischief in his voice. "Let him go. His car's in the pound. Oh, and, by the way, you'll have to apologize. It seems that when our officer was moving the Porsche, Mr Loscoe's mobile phone got broken."

Neil smiled. Clare began to work out what game they were playing, and smiled too.

As Loscoe left, Eddie Broom's solicitor arrived. He went through the line-up arrangements with Greasby.

"My client has not been charged with anything?"

"No."

"So, as soon as your witness fails to identify him, you release him."

"Presuming he isn't identified, yes."

There was a big buzz around the station as Candia Arnold came in. Even though she looked jet-lagged, with lank hair and crumpled clothes, every head in the building turned when the supermodel walked by. Candia was angry about having to come to Nottingham the moment she got back to Birmingham, and wanted to be out as quickly as possible. Phil Church, the Solihull DC accompanying her, kept apologizing. He looked out of his depth.

"What's this guy's alibi for the night of the burglary?" he asked.

"Staying with a girlfriend."

"She backs him up?"

"I'm sure she will," Clare said. "But the woman's daughter was interviewed two days after the burglary and said that there'd been no one staying over." She'd got this snippet from Ben at the party last night. Only problem was, there was no way of verifying it because Ben was basking on a beach for ten days.

The solicitor came out from seeing his client and pronounced himself satisfied that all the proprieties of an identification parade had been observed. Eddie joined the line-up.

"Take your time," DI Greasby told Candia Arnold.

But she didn't. The model walked up and down the line twice, then turned to the DI.

"He's not there."

"I take it you'll be releasing Mr Broom immediately?" the solicitor asked Greasby afterwards.

"After he's told us his whereabouts on the nights of the previous ten burglaries."

"Nine," the solicitor said. "My client is of the impression that no burglary took place at the Loscoe house last week."

"So he said. Nine, then."

The solicitor took the list of dates and returned, nearly an hour later, with a list of names and addresses. Clare scanned it at the same time as Paul and DI Greasby. Each alibi looked cast-iron. There were at least two people who'd seen him on each occasion and he was a long way from the site of each burglary.

"All right," Greasby said, taking the list. "We'll check these, of course, but we'll also release Mr Broom immediately. Apologize to him for the inconvenience."

"You're only doing your job," the solicitor assured him.

"And making a complete hash of it," Clare heard DC Church mutter under his breath, before he took the list of alibis back to Birmingham with Candia Arnold.

"I've never seen a list of alibis as thorough as that," Greasby told the others, when they were alone in the CID offices.

"Me neither," Paul Grace agreed. "Makes you think that he knew when the burglaries were going to be and made sure he was well out of the way. Question is, how do we prove it?"

"Not our problem," Greasby told him. "Let the boys in Birmingham deal with it. We've enough tough cases of our own."

Paul said nothing, only looked at Clare, who looked back at him. She knew that expression. It was like seeing her own face in a mirror. He'd caught a bug and wouldn't be happy until he'd tracked down the motorway team and put them away. Which meant that Clare wouldn't be happy, either.

She would give anything if they could break the case together.

20

Neil sat by the tape machine, waiting. The phone tap had been authorized, but that didn't mean he would find out anything. Eddie might decide to go and see Gordon, and the tap would be a waste of time. Neil didn't like waiting. He kept thinking about Clare spending the night with Inspector Grace. He didn't want to, but he couldn't stop himself.

An hour after Eddie's release, Gordon's phone rang. The call came from a mobile number.

"What do you think you're playing at?" Eddie asked him.

"They put me in a spot, Eddie. They think the robbery was faked."

"Yeah," Eddie said. "Because it was. Only you tried to put the blame on me."

"That's not true."

"Don't bullshit me, Gordon. I heard the tape."

"I ... um. There must be a misunderstanding."

"You bet there is. I don't have an alibi for that night. You got me arrested, you half-wit."

"I'm sorry, Eddie. It won't –"

"Too bloody right it won't. Ring me back on your mobile."

"I can't. It's knackered."

Neil waited. Eddie probably knew better than to incriminate himself on a British Telecom line. But he was angry, and angry people sometimes said stupid things.

"All right," Eddie said. "Listen carefully. You're going to see your solicitor and confess to faking the burglary."

"Eddie?" Gordon's voice pleaded.

"You made the robbery up after reading about the gang in the papers, that's what you'll say. Withdraw your insurance claim, plead poverty and, if you're lucky, you might avoid prison time. That's my advice to you, Gordon."

"I can't –"

"You want to hear the alternative? The alternative is that your body will never be found. Understood?"

There was a silence before Gordon grunted his reply.

"Yeah."

Eddie hung up. Neil yelled for Inspector Greasby.

"Gotta go, sweetheart."

"When'll you be back, Eddie?" Shirley asked.

"Your guess is as good as mine. Here."

He peeled some notes from his wallet.

"In case the Lottery money doesn't arrive."

"You won't come on holiday with us?"

"Better not. Got to make myself scarce for a few days – just to be on the safe side. If I'm with you, the police'll know where to find me."

Eddie gave Julie a kiss, then little Tammy, then slapped Curt on the back.

"I'd keep out of that newsagent's if I were you," he told him.

They went out into the street to wave him off. Eddie opened the door of his Merc.

"I'm gonna have to change this motor," he said. "Pity."

He drove off to wherever it was he went. Curt's eyes were full of admiration.

"When I grow up," Curt told Julie, "I wanna be just like him."

Gordon Loscoe gave himself up later that afternoon. Neil took his statement. Loscoe admitted committing the fraud because he didn't have enough money to settle his debts. He pleaded with the police not to prosecute Maxine or Natalie.

"I pressured them into it," he explained. "But it wasn't their fault. I blew all the money."

"You're really broke?" Neil asked.

"I'll be clear if I sell the house," the former millionaire said. "But I needed money fast – school fees, council tax, fuel bills. They eat away at you."

He had, he reckoned, gambled away two million pounds in two years, and spent the rest.

"What about the motorway team?" Neil asked DI Greasby, after Loscoe had been taken into custody for a second night. "Aren't the Task Force going to follow Eddie Broom? He's obviously one of them."

"With his ten terrific alibis?" the Inspector said, sardonically. "It might be obvious to you, but they seem to think that we're fantasizing."

"He's connected somehow," Neil argued.

"I agree," Greasby said. "And I'll make sure that Solihull know what we found out. But I think we'll have trouble convincing them that Eddie Broom is the criminal mastermind behind the motorway burglaries rather than just a hard man who had a falling-out with a friend."

"Where does that leave us?"

"He's left Nottingham. He's not our problem."

The Inspector looked at his watch.

"It's five. That's seven hours' overtime. I can't afford to authorize any more. Go home."

In Paul Grace's kitchen, Clare cooked penne with

broccoli and pine nuts.

"That was some birthday yesterday," Paul said, opening the wine.

"The best."

"Want to go to the casino again next weekend?"

"Sorry," Clare said, diplomatically. "I enjoyed last night, but it's still not me."

"Do you know how much money we won?"

"You won it, not me."

Paul ignored this comment.

"Those were high minimum stakes on that table. I got enough to pay for a good little holiday – a weekend in Paris, say, or Amsterdam."

"I'd like that," Clare said.

"Or we could go somewhere for longer. I'm due three weeks' holiday, and you've got at least two. How do you fancy Florida, or San Francisco?"

Clare put a finger to his lips.

"I fancy it," she said, "and I fancy you. But I don't have that much money and I don't want to rush things. Let's start with a weekend away."

"You're on," Paul said, putting his arms around her from behind and kissing her neck, making her feel all warm inside. "I'll sort something out soon."

The next morning, Paul was on earlies. He kissed Clare goodbye at twenty to six. Clare rolled over and pulled the duvet tightly around her, but couldn't get back to sleep. Her life was changing so fast. She had a new job and a new lover. She was bursting with happiness. But she was also nervous. There'd been times before when everything seemed to be going right, when life had turned around and kicked her in the teeth. She didn't want it to happen again. But if you didn't take a chance, you never won. That's what Paul would say. You made your own luck. So maybe it was Clare's turn to win. Maybe, where men were concerned, it would be third time lucky.

Clare got up, had a shower, then drove home to put on some fresh clothes. She was at work before everybody else, which was how she came to answer the phone when it rang, five minutes before she was meant to be on duty.

"This is the National Lottery security section, returning DC Foster's call on Friday."

"He's not in yet," Clare said. "Perhaps I can help."

As things had turned out, there'd been no need for the call. Neil had been looking for a link between Gordon Loscoe, Eddie Broom and Julie Wilder that didn't exist.

"DC Foster wanted to know if there were any suspicious circumstances around the winning scratch card bought by a member of the Wilder family the Friday before last."

"Actually…"

Clare was about to say that it didn't matter, but

kept her mouth shut. Crimes had been committed and, while CID might not choose to pursue them, she couldn't cover them up, either.

"The thing is, we've decided not to pay out on the scratch card."

"Why not?" Clare asked.

"There was a phone call last week, from, I believe, a disgruntled ex-boyfriend of the claimant. He claimed that the ticket was really bought by the claimant's younger brother, who is only fifteen. We get this sort of malicious call quite often, but when I rang the newsagent who sold the ticket, his replies were – to say the least – suspicious. He thought that the prize had already been paid and further questioning produced a garbled story. I suspected that the newsagent might be colluding with the claimant, Ms Wilder."

"I see," Clare said.

She felt sorry for Julie, but Clare couldn't deny the story. Curt *had* bought the ticket.

"We sent an investigator round on Friday. He spoke to various people on the Maynard Estate and came back with stories about beatings up, people being hit by cars, even – and I'm sure this is an exaggeration – guns. Frankly, we're surprised that the police didn't get in touch with us earlier."

Clare said nothing.

"So, we've written to Ms Wilder telling her that she doesn't qualify for the prize. And the newsagent, Mr Singh, will lose his franchise to sell Lottery tickets."

"But you haven't proved that the boy bought the ticket," Clare argued.

"We don't need to."

"Why not?" Clare asked. "Surely the girl won fifty thousand pounds? And, when it comes down to it, does it matter who bought the scratch card? You got the pound stake. The money for the prize is in your budget."

There was a short silence.

"To be honest with you," the woman said, "it's all about publicity. We judge that the headlines will be worse if we pay out and then the true story appears in the press, than if we don't, and Ms Wilder sues us."

"It does seem cruel," Clare argued. "I'm sure lots of people get away with what the Wilders did."

"I'm sure they do."

"Couldn't you give them some kind of settlement?"

"No, that would be to admit liability. It's all or nothing. You sound very concerned. Are these people friends of yours?"

"No," Clare said, "but I've met them. They're very badly off. I feel sorry for them, that's all."

"I know," the anonymous voice on the other end of the phone said, "but in this life, there are winners and losers. Sorry. Goodbye."

Epilogue

The Lottery office had promised to phone on Monday. Julie needed the cheque by Tuesday, or there wouldn't be time for the money to clear and for her to pay for the holiday, flying out on Sunday.

"Can Natalie come with us?" Curt asked.

"I'll think about it," Julie said.

Natalie was sitting on the sofa with her arm around Julie's brother, wearing the posh green uniform of the High School. Today, she was skiving off. Her dad was going to prison, the police said. Her mum might be, but would most probably get away with a suspended sentence. Natalie wasn't being prosecuted, but she was going to have to leave her posh school. Her family couldn't afford the fees.

"Maybe we'll move back round here," Natalie

was saying. "Maybe I can go to the same school as you."

Curt hadn't told her that he wasn't at an actual school, but a referral unit. Still, he was only just beginning his GCSE year. Maybe there was time for him to change. If he behaved, the teachers said last term, Curt might just get into a proper school somewhere, and take his exams. Until now, he'd shown no interest. But Curt had changed over the past two weeks. Being beaten up had shaken him. Getting off with Natalie had made him less bitter. And being with Uncle Eddie had made him more ambitious – though Julie didn't like to think what ambitions Eddie might have instilled in him. Maybe Curt could begin again.

Maybe *she* could.

The phone rang. Mum was still in bed, so Julie answered it.

"This is Clare Coppola, from CID. Look, I don't know how to tell you this, but I guess you'd rather hear it from me than in a letter –"

The DC told Julie the news she'd been secretly expecting all along. Julie watched Natalie as she listened. The girl was playing with Tammy. Curt was beaming at them both, the happiest she'd seen him for years.

"Thanks for telling me," Julie said, when the DC had finished her explanation. "It was good of you to call."

Dave had done it. Her ex-boyfriend had worked out that Curt had bought the ticket and told the Lottery people. When she told Curt, he would go ballistic.

The policewoman was still talking, apologizing, trying to make it right.

"No," Julie said, stopping her. "It's all right. We'll get by without it."

She put the phone down and looked at Curt, concern beginning to spread across his face. She thought of what would happen if she told him about Dave. One attack would lead to another, then another...

"The Lottery?" Curt asked.

Julie nodded.

"That was the police. The Italian girl. She didn't want to tell the Lottery people the truth about you buying the ticket, but a senior officer overruled her. We're not going to get any money."

Natalie burst into tears and hugged Curt.

"It's all right," Curt told Natalie. "It's only money. We don't need it, anyway. All it's brought is bad luck. Look at what it did to your dad."

Julie felt ... not loss, exactly, but numbness. Then came a kind of relief. It was over. Upstairs, she heard Mum going into the bathroom.

"Who was that on the phone?" she shouted down.

"I'll tell you in a minute!" Julie yelled back,

dreading her mum's reaction, trying to think of how she'd tell her, then giving up. Let Curt do it. He bought the bloody ticket in the first place.

Julie went into the kitchen to put the kettle on. They were out of teabags, so she'd have to reuse two from the saucer on the sink. There was a damp breeze blowing from outside, the first sign of autumn. Julie closed the kitchen window then smelt the milk, to make sure that it wasn't off. A police-car siren sounded and Julie looked out of the window to find out what was going on.

All she could see was an Intercity train leaving the station, white blinds cloaking the first-class carriages at its front. Well-off people were on their way to London, to shop, or to work. Julie imagined their luxurious lives. What would they feel, those people, in their comfortable railway carriages, if they looked down on the Maynard Estate? Contempt? Pity? Fear? Or, more likely, nothing at all? *It could be you*, she thought to herself, as the train passed into the distance.

In the living room, Tammy began to cry.